THE BURIED CHRISTMAS

DENNIS BAILEY

THE BOY WHO CRIED CHRISTMAS by Dennis Bailey

ISBN: 978-0-578-77054-3

Copyright © 2020 by Dennis Bailey
Cover design by Darko Tomic

Available in print and ebook from your local bookstore, online, or from the author at: www.dennisbaileyauthor.com

For more information on this book and the author, visit:
http://www.dennisbaileyauthor.com/

Library of Congress Cataloging-in-Publication Data
Bailey, Dennis
The Boy Who Cried Christmas / Dennis Bailey

Printed in the United States of America

For Hugh Mitchell

Who so looked forward to reading this novel,
only to be called home by the Lord before it was
completed.

ACKNOWLEDGMENTS

I want to thank my Father in heaven, His Son, Jesus, and the Holy Spirit for their gift of a third career, this time as an author, and for the calling and priviledge to serve Them with my writing. For what better job can a man have in this life than to write about his God?

To my wife, Lee, the love of my life and biggest supporter of my writing career. Thank you for all you do to take care of me, our home, and our family so that I can follow my dream of becoming a writer.

Lastly, to my friend, mentor, editor, writing coach, and varsity cheerleader, DiAnn Mills. Renowned author of over fifty-five books, where would I be without your invaluable help and encouragement over the years? Little did I know what was in store for me when I accepted your invitation to join your Craftsman writing class nine years ago in Dallas.

CHAPTER 1

Present Day
December 20

Nine-year-old Logan Ailshie waited while his mother paused to gaze in another storefront window on W 45th Street. His patience tested, he resisted the urge to whine, fearing she might decide to end their shopping spree before they got to the Disney Store. There she'd purchase gifts for him, and return his accelerated pulse to normal.

They'd spent most of the morning shopping on 5th Avenue. Some Italian place to find a suit for his stepdad, a fancy makeup store called Sephora, then to pick up a sixteen-hundred-dollar handbag for his aunt. It didn't look like much to him, but his mom seemed quite impressed the initials LV had been printed all over the bag. After another minute, she turned from the window, grabbed Logan by the hand, and continued west toward Times Square. Although he'd reached the age where he didn't think it was necessary for her to hold his hand, he didn't really mind so much. His mom was super pretty, and the attention she drew from other men and women on the street made him feel proud.

To him, the streets of Manhattan looked like one big commercial for Santa Claus. Less than a week before Christmas, displays of the jolly old fat man, Christmas trees, and winter wonderlands populated every storefront window. Each presentation was made more appealing by the elaborate strings of lights bordering the outside. Like most kids, Logan loved the decorations. But turning the city into a second North Pole was only part of the reason. Decorations signaled the start of the countdown to his receiving everything on his gift list. Directly in front of them, a huge billboard hung on the side of a building that read: Make America Great Again, Skip Church! Nearing the corner, his ears picked up the familiar ring of a Salvation Army bell by a middle-aged man standing next to one of the famous red kettles.

Logan and his mom made a right onto Broadway where they entered the Disney Store. He led her to a line of shelves containing toys and other stuff based on the *Incredibles 2* animated movie, a picture he'd seen four times.

"Here they are, Mom." He picked up several items, including an *Incredibles* logo T-shirt, a Mr. Incredible action figure, and a set of character drinking cups.

"Are you sure you got everything you wanted? You didn't leave anything behind, did you?"

Logan recognized his mother's sarcasm. And although he may have felt a twinge of guilt at being so greedy, it wasn't enough to cause him to put anything back.

His mom looked down at him with raised eyebrows. "You do realize Christmas is more than just about you getting presents?"

If it was, his parents hadn't done much to reinforce

the notion. His stepfather, a successful Wall Street executive, married his mom when Logan was three. Together, the three of them lived in a fancy East 63rd Street condominium. To make up for never being around or showing much interest in Logan, his stepdad tried to compensate by buying him everything he wanted. This was particularly true at Christmastime. As far back as he could remember, he never had less than twenty presents under the tree with his name on them.

While they waited for the cashier, Logan pleaded with his mom to wear the *Incredibles* T-shirt out of the store.

Mom crossed her arms and lowered her chin. "How's Santa going to bring it to you if you're already wearing it?"

Logan rolled his eyes. "Oh, come on, Mom. I learned last year you and Dad are Santa Claus."

"You'll still have to wait until Christmas before wearing it."

"Why?"

"Because it's a Christmas present and it's not Christmas yet."

Logan gritted his teeth. "Fine." He grabbed the T-shirt off the counter and threw it onto the floor.

His mom threw her hands to her hips. "Pick that up, young man," she said, a sternness in her voice.

"No." Logan pressed his lips tightly together and stomped back to the *Incredibles* display.

"Logan, get over here."

He kept his back to her, pretending not to hear.

"Logan."

He peeked back over his shoulder but stood firm. Mom apologized to the cashier, picked up the T-shirt, and paid for the items. She approached him and asked if he wanted to carry the bag, but he just shook his head. "I'll take you to Chick-Fil-A."

Here it comes. Every time he'd get mad at her or refused to do something she wanted, she'd pull out the old Chick-Fil-A card as a bribe. Usually, he was too weak to resist, especially with a Chick-Fil-A right around the corner. Sometimes he regretted letting her know how much he loved their chicken nuggets. "Okay, but I'm still not carrying the bag."

After lunch, Logan exited the fast food restaurant carrying what was left of his soda and waffle-cut fries. Just north of the exit, a homeless man held a cardboard sign that read, "Hungry Veteran Needs Help." The man looked to be in his thirties, clean-shaven, and had a military-style haircut. He wore a green army jacket. A small red Christmas ball about the size of a quarter dangled from one of the buttonholes in his coat. Logan approached the man and offered him the fries.

"Why thank you, young man," he said, "But I sure could use something to wash them down with."

Logan handed him the soda.

His mom walked up beside Logan and put her arm around his shoulder. "I think we've taken up enough of this man's time, sweetie. And we still have a great deal of shopping to do."

The man thanked him again before adding, "Your mom's right, though. Christmas is more than just about getting presents."

As they walked away, Logan looked back over his shoulder at the man. *How did he know about that?*

"That was very generous," Mom said.

"I remember what you and Dad told me about our

country's veterans. Besides, the man really did look hungry."

They turned right onto W 47th Street and made their way back to 5th Avenue to shop for another two hours before taking a taxi home.

No sooner had they arrived than Logan pressed her again about wearing the t-shirt. When she refused to give in, he stormed into his room, slammed the door, and flipped on the TV. Twice she'd told him no, but he wasn't about to give up. He'd get that t-shirt one way or another. And he wasn't about to wait until Christmas. He just needed to push the right buttons.

Following dinner, while Mom loaded the dishwasher, Logan spotted his dad on the couch in the living room. He'd been reading a report he brought home from work. After spending all day shopping with his mom, Logan was in the mood for some guy talk. "Hey, Dad. How about a game of Stratego?"

Dad stared at the pamphlet on his lap. "Not tonight, Logan. Maybe tomorrow."

Logan kneeled beside the Christmas tree decorated with white lights and blue and silver balls standing a few feet away in the corner. He examined the packages beneath it in search of ones with his name on them. When he found one, he'd pick it up and give it a shake. One smaller box drew special attention. "I wonder if this is my new iPhone?"

His mom entered the living room. "What makes you think you're getting one?"

Logan grinned broadly. "Dad. I heard today the Yankees are already talking about choosing Gerrit Cole to pitch on opening day. Do you think we might be able to go to the game?"

His dad ignored him.

Logan felt his heart sink. "Dad?"

"I'm trying to read this prospectus, Logan. Let's talk later."

Mom put a hand on his shoulder. "I'll play Stratego with you if you want."

While he'd played with her before, he didn't consider her as worthy an opponent as his stepdad. "No thanks. I think I'll just go to my room." Logan paused on his way out of the living room and turned back to him. "Goodnight, Dad."

His stepfather grunted, never looking up from the report.

Logan entered his bedroom and felt a chill. He hit the light switch and closed the door behind him. Burr. *Where's that draft coming from?* Across the room, one of the two windows was cracked open about four inches. Strange. He hadn't had a reason to open the window. Not in this weather. Could Mom have been in here cleaning and forgot to shut it? He shut the window, but needed a sweatshirt from his closet. He took a step inside the darkened space and a hand clasped over his mouth. A man pulled him in close and whispered in his ear. "I'm not here to hurt you, just to talk. Do you understand?"

Legs shaking, Logan managed a nod.

"If I take my hand away, will you promise not to cry out?"

A yell would immediately bring his parents into the room, but there was something calming about the man's voice, some supernatural quality he didn't understand. His legs stopped shaking. He decided to trust him, nodding again.

"Let's get out of this closet." With his hand still

over Logan's mouth, the man marched him out of the closet and over to his bed where he let him sit.

Logan stared into the man's face. Before him stood the person he'd given his lunch to earlier in the afternoon. Logan pointed at him. 'You're . . . you're." His finger moved from his face to the little red ball hanging from his buttonhole. "That homeless guy from this afternoon."

"Robert is my name."

"But how did you get in here?"

Robert put his finger over his mouth. "Shh. We need to keep our voices down. I came in through the window."

"What do you mean, the window. We're on the 10th floor." Logan didn't know a whole lot about the law of gravity and physics, but he knew enough to know that only Spiderman could have climbed up the outside of the building. And this guy was no Spiderman.

"That's okay. I'm not afraid of heights."

"So why are you here? Are you some kind of angel or something?"

Robert's head jerked back slightly. "Very good. That's pretty perceptive for a boy your age. What made you say that?"

"Process of elimination. I already figured out you weren't Spiderman. And I can't think of another human being crazy enough to try and make the climb up here. Plus, that business with you knowing what my mom said to me in the Disney Store this morning. So let's see. Defies gravity. Picks locks. Reads minds. My guess is an angel."

"Speaking of this morning, have you given any thought to what your mother said?"

"You mean about Christmas being more than about me getting presents?"

"There is a more profound meaning, you know?"

"You mean Jesus? Oh yeah, everybody's heard that story before."

"Then you know how important His birth was?"

"Well, sure. If Jesus hadn't been born, there wouldn't *be* a Christmas, and there wouldn't be any presents."

Robert smiled and shook his head. "I can see you still have quite a bit to learn. How much do you know about the birth of Jesus?"

"Just what I learned in Sunday school. That a couple named Mary and Joseph traveled to a town called Bethlehem. That Mary had to have her baby in a stable because there was no room for them in the inn. And after Jesus was born, they laid him in a manger. And that a star led three wise men to the place where He was born."

"Do you believe it?"

"Oh, I don't know. My mom does, but my stepfather says it's all hooey. So do a lot of my friends at school. I guess I really never thought about it much."

"Would you like to know for certain who's right?"

Logan thought for a second. "I guess so, but I don't know how anyone could ever be certain of anything they hadn't seen with their own eyes."

"Excellent point. What do you say we test out your theory?"

"How?"

"Are you game for taking a little journey?"

Logan couldn't believe he was considering saying yes. Ten minutes ago he'd found a stranger hiding in his closet, and now he was thinking of going on a trip with the guy. But the truth was, Robert could have hurt him at any time but he didn't. Instead, he showed a quiet strength and a gentleness that convinced Logan he was the real thing. The way Logan saw it, if he couldn't trust an angel, who could he trust? "How long are we going to be gone?"

"Just long enough to prove your theory."

"Okay."

"You might want to grab a coat. It's chilly out tonight."

Logan grabbed his coat from the closet and followed him to the window. Robert raised one of the panes and took the boy by the hand. "Ready?" he said.

CHAPTER 2

Seated on the edge of his bed, FBI Special Agent in Charge Marcus Garraway peered down the barrel of his Glock 19M auto pistol. On the comforter next to him, his cell phone rang incessantly. But Marcus was too fixated to tolerate interruption and continued to examine the bullet seated at the far end of the darkened barrel. If he held the gun at the precise angle, he could just make out the groves cut into the brass jacketed hollow point about to enter his brain.

On an adjacent nightstand, his deceased wife, Carolyn smiled at him from within the frame of an eight by ten photograph. Two years ago this Christmas Eve, she was driving home in light snow along the Taconic State Parkway following a visit to her parents in Albany. A drunk traveling on the wrong side of the road struck her head on, killing her instantly.

Carolyn had always loved Christmas for what she always held was its true meaning, a celebration of the birth of Jesus Christ. And during their ten-year marriage, she made every effort to influence her husband into accepting that premise. Marcus, on the other hand, while genuinely stirred by his wife's faith, was content to adhere to a more secular commemoration of the holiday. Sure, he said and did all the right things to support his wife's beliefs, even agreed to accompany her to church on occasion, especially on Christmas Eve. But when it got right down to it, he had trouble accepting anything as ridiculous as the concept of a virgin birth. His background and training as a law enforcement officer—analytical, skeptical, pragmatic—simply wouldn't allow it.

Still, knowing his doubts, his wife never gave up hope he'd one day come to know Christ and was determined to set a good example. In addition to church every Sunday, she hosted a women's Bible study in their home on Wednesday evenings, volunteered at the local YWCA, and insisted on saying grace before every meal. For his fortieth birthday, she presented him with his first-ever copy of the Bible and included an inscription inside the front cover. He even opened it a couple of times, although admittedly more out of curiosity than a quest for salvation.

But even his curiosity died with Carolyn that dark Christmas Eve, along with any interest he might have had in celebrating the holiday. Worse yet, he'd come to hate Christmas and anything associated with it. To have his wife die on the eve of the day she loved more than any other was an irony too painful to bear. And one he was determined to silence.

Marcus looked down into the barrel again. He took a swig from the bottle of Jack Daniels cradled between his legs and put the gun into his mouth. Similar to the taste of a zinc pill he once bit into, the taste of blued steel and gun oil tainted the flavor of the whiskey. He reached for the trigger and recalled how much he didn't want to be remembered as just another cop who'd "eaten his gun." He despised that idiom. Instead, he pressed the barrel against his right temple and inserted his finger into the trigger guard.

Startled by the ding of a text message, he jerked and nearly pulled the trigger. Marcus turned the gun aside and reached for his phone. Between the liquor and the tears welling his eyes, he struggled to read.

The text came from Janice Fowlkes, one of his team members.

Why aren't you answering your phone? 9-year-old boy missing, possible kidnapping. Respond immediately.

Marcus tried to ignore the message. After all, a slight pressure on the trigger meant an end to all his pain, depression, loneliness, and yes, responsibility for other people's lives. Just a clean-up job for his apartment building's custodian. *A nine-year-old boy.* He swore.

He worked in the FBI's regional Child Abduction Response Deployment (CARD) team, an elite group of seasoned professionals specializing in the investigation of crimes against children cases. They focused on the recovery of missing children and the apprehension of those responsible for taking them.

He removed the magazine from the pistol and ejected the chambered round, then put the cap on the liquor bottle and set it on the night stand. He called Janice, grabbed his coat, and took one more glance at the nightstand before heading out the door. Fortunately, Jack was still half full, assuring upon his return he could pick up where he left off.

* * *

"You can open your eyes now," Robert said.

Logan heard the words but couldn't make his

eyelids obey. Back in his room, fully expecting to drop ten stories, he'd closed his eyes and grabbed Robert's arm before they stepped through the window. But when his foot left the window sill, it landed immediately on what felt like solid, or at the very least, sandy ground. At the same time, the stench of some unknown, unwashed animal assaulted his nose, along with the sound of several others grunting off to his right.

"And you can let go of my arm, too."

Logan opened his eyes and released Robert's arm. Twenty yards to their left stood a large tent that didn't look like it was made for camping. Next to it, a man dressed in Arab clothing tended a torch illuminating the outside. Logan sucked in a breath. They stood in the middle of a vast desert wasteland. To their right, eight camels lay on the desert floor tied to stakes. Logan checked the time on his *Incredibles 2* digital watch—8:35 p.m. Yep. Either he was hallucinating or Robert must be a real angel.

"Stay here," Robert said. "I'll be right back." He turned, his black combat boots kicking up sand as he walked.

"Wait a minute." Logan sensed a pang of fear. "Where are we?" He scanned the area again looking for clues to their whereabouts, but all he saw was sand and stars in every direction. Arizona, he guessed. Maybe the Nevada desert. But then, what's with the camels and the man dressed like an Arab? Were they part of some circus act?

Robert spoke to the Arab, and from the sound of things, his new friend appeared to be working some kind of a deal with him. A few minutes later, he returned nodding his head. "Looks like we've got a ride."

Logan looked for a car or truck. "What ride?"

Robert pointed to the camels. "Those."

A camel? Logan had never even been on a horse before. Did they bite? Would they buck him off? "Couldn't we maybe find a Jeep or a Humvee?"

"Out here? I don't think so." Robert chuckled. "Besides, these are better for traveling in the desert. Let's go." Robert boosted the boy onto one of the animals.

"Why are you putting me on while he's still on the ground?" The camel's body felt solid against Logan's legs. He checked both sides looking for stirrups to put his feet in, but couldn't find any.

"You'll see. Grab that saddle horn with both hands and hold on tight. The camel will get up using its back legs first, so be sure to lean back a little until it raises its front legs." Robert coaxed the animal to its feet by lifting its bridle.

The camel let out a loud grunt, which sounded like a cross between a burp and a goose's honk. "Now you've done it. You made him mad." Despite being jostled, Logan managed to stay upright in the saddle.

"Not mad. Just irritated."

"Don't camels spit?"

"Not spitting, actually. More like throwing up."

"Oh, great. What am I going to tell my parents if I come home with camel puke all over my clothes?"

"Just keep your distance when you're in front of them and you won't have anything to worry about." Robert mounted his camel, and the two rode away from the encampment. Fortunately, a three-quarter moon provided just enough light for them to travel by.

A little more than an hour later they went around a large body of water. Along the way, Logan had grasped fairly well the art of camel-riding. Although a little bouncy, he'd learned how to shift his weight in the saddle in rhythm with the animal's stride.

"What's this?" Logan said.

"The Salt Sea. I believe today it's better known as the Dead Sea."

"The Dead Sea. Isn't that somewhere in the Middle East?"

"Very good. I see someone hasn't been sleeping through his world geography class."

Whoa! From New York to the Middle East in the blink of an eye. Even the transporter aboard the Starship Enterprise couldn't have gotten them there that fast. But why the Middle East? And how would being there prove anything?

At least the camel ride was cool. Logan hadn't had so much fun since his mom put him on his first carousel when he was four. Only the horse on that ride could only go up and down and around in circles. This ride was not only more gratifying, but included a view of the star-filled sky above the water.

December 21

With the sun coming up on their backs, Logan and Robert sat on their mounts overlooking a hilltop and several herds of sheep. "Down there," Robert said, "you'll find some men to help you."

"Help me with what? Aren't you coming?"

"I have a short errand to run. But don't worry, I'll be around."

Logan was having second thoughts about accepting

Robert's invitation. No sooner had he begun to trust the man who'd safely brought him to a foreign land than he was abandoning him with strangers. "Who are they?"

"Shepherds."

Logan looked at men dressed in strange clothing. Some sat around a fire, and shadows of others stood near the sheep. "How can they help me?"

"Seek a man named Simeon. He will tell you all you need to know." Robert turned his camel and started back down the other side of the hill. "Good luck."

"Wait a minute," Logan said. "How am I supposed to know —"

"Seek out Simeon."

CHAPTER 3

At 10:34 p.m., Agent Garraway entered the Thomas apartment, where he met with Agent Fowlkes and another CARD team member, Agent Todd Curtis. Agent Fowlkes sported long blonde hair and dressed in a conservative gray business suit. Agent Curtis, a male in his forties, wore a green polo shirt under his brown sport jacket. Two uniformed NYPD officers stood guard near the entrance.

Todd and Janice gave their supervisor a quick rundown of the circumstances surrounding the case.

I'll introduce you to Logan's parents," Janice said.

A woman wearing a beige robe sat on the living room couch sobbing against the chest of a man who Marcus assumed was her husband. The man, an inch or two shorter than Marcus's six feet, stood when the agents approached, extending his hand to the supervisor. "I'm Brad Thomas. Thank you for coming out, although frankly I don't understand what purpose having the FBI here serves."

"For one thing, access to additional resources, Mr. Thomas. Also, my team specializes in investigating cases involving missing children.

A man in a charcoal jacket with a NYPD detective's badge hanging from his breast pocket walked from a bedroom to their left. "Agent Garraway?" He extended his hand.

The two men shook hands. "I'm Garraway."

"Sean Mahoney, Missing Persons Squad." He pointed to the room he'd exited. "I think what you'll want to see is in here."

Marcus lowered his voice to a whisper. "All right. Just give me a minute with the parents." He introduced himself to the couple on the couch, and after a brief conversation headed to the bedroom.

When he entered, the first thing he noticed — besides the two NYPD crime scene technicians dusting for fingerprints — was the fully opened window. Other than that, nothing in the room appeared out of place, no signs of a struggle. He pointed to the open window while addressing Detective Mahoney. "That's the way you found it?"

"Just like that." Mahoney gestured to the technicians. "Other than these guys, nobody's touched it since we got here."

Marcus walked to the opening and placed his hands in his pockets. He leaned his head out the window, being careful not to touch anything. "Whew." He stepped back in. "That's a heck of a drop. I assume you checked the roof? No ropes, wire, or evidence anything else was used to hoist the boy up?"

"Lots of pigeon dung," Detective Mahoney said. That's it. And we searched the entire building, including the garage, storage units, utility closets, even the elevator shafts."

Marcus nodded. "Good. Let's search it again."

He exited the bedroom, sat down in a chair next to the Thomases, and pulled out a notebook. "I know this has been tough on you, but do you feel up to answering a few more questions?"

Mrs. Thomas lifted her head off her husband's chest and wiped her eyes with a tissue. "Sure. Whatever we can do to help you find our son."

"Logan's biological father. Where is he?"

"His name is David Ailshie, and he lives in Hawaii," Mrs. Thomas said. "He hasn't seen or spoken to Logan since we divorced six years ago."

"Is there any chance he might have tried to make contact with the boy without your knowledge?"

"I seriously doubt it. In six years, he hasn't sent Logan so much as a birthday or Christmas card."

Marcus turned his attention to her husband. "And how is your relationship with Logan, Mr. Thomas. Any stepparent issues?"

"I've been the only father Logan has known since he was three. He calls me Dad. So, no, there aren't any issues."

"Has the boy ever run away before?"

"Never," Mrs. Thomas said.

"When was the last time you had an argument?"

"This morning, when we were out shopping, he got mad because I wouldn't let him have one of his Christmas presents early." She stood and took two steps away from the couch before wheeling around. "But I'm telling you, he didn't run away. Both my husband and I watched him walk into that bedroom after dinner and never come out. In fact, I only learned he was missing because I felt a draft coming from beneath his door when I walked past on the way to bed. And when I went in to check, the window was open and he was gone."

"And you're certain there's no way he could have slipped past you and gotten out the front door?"

"Positive."

Marcus tried his best not to prejudge. He genuinely liked the Thomases and thought they'd exhibited the proper amount of concern for parents suffering the loss of a child. But he'd also investigated enough cases with similar inexplicable means of disappearance to know in most instances the parents were involved. Still, he didn't want to put them on the defensive by accusing them outright. Instead, he'd just give them a little rope. He noticed a telephone sitting on an end table next to the couch. "I see you have a hardline telephone here."

"We keep it as a safeguard in case the cell towers go down."

"Good. In the event this does turn out to be an abduction, I'm going to leave Todd and Janice here tonight to install and monitor wiretap and tracing equipment on your home phone."

The Thomases nodded.

"And for the foreseeable future, they'll be an agent posted at your husband's office and two more assigned to shadow each of you should you receive a call on your cell phone. They'll be able to monitor the call and assist you with your response in real time."

Mr. Thomas's face tightened. "They won't have to go into the bathroom with us, will they?"

"Not unless you take your cell phone in with you."

"What about posting a reward?"

"Not yet. That's something we may want to consider later on down the road, but for now we should wait to see if anyone contacts you. Posting a reward brings all kinds of kooks out of the woodwork and tends to generate a lot of false leads. One more thing—I assume you have a recent photograph of

Logan we could borrow, but would you also have a copy of his fingerprints?"

"Yes," Mrs. Thomas said. "Last year Logan's school hosted a 'Fingerprint your Child Day' in conjunction with our local precinct."

"Excellent. I'd like to get those from you before I leave. It will help with the investigation."

"Of course."

Mrs. Thomas returned to the couch and again fell against her husband's chest and cried.

"Look," Marcus said, "I know you probably won't be getting much sleep tonight. But try to remember there are nearly forty thousand police officers and another two thousand FBI agents in this city, all out looking for your son."

After receiving Logan's photo and fingerprint card, Marcus met with Todd and Janice in the foyer to issue instructions for setting up the wiretap equipment.

"What do you think?" Todd said.

Marcus sighed heavily. "I don't know yet." He flipped back a couple of pages to review his notes. "But I'll tell you what I don't think. I don't think that kid flew out the window."

CHAPTER 4

Logan had little difficulty locating Simeon, who was one of four adult shepherds watching their flocks in the area, and the second one he came to. An older man with gray hair and a beard, he wasn't dressed the way Logan had expected of a modern day sheepherder. He carried a crook and wore a long gray tunic with an off-white cloth covering his head like the shepherds he'd seen in a movie about the Nativity with his mom. The other shepherds dressed the same. They included Eliab and his two teenage sons, Perez and Asher, Jachin and his teenage son, Ephraim, and Zephon, who traveled alone. Logan was so relieved to find they spoke English. Their accents were strong, but at least they could understand each other.

Simeon invited Logan to join him and the others in their camp for a breakfast of dates, goat's milk, and flat bread. Famished, Logan reached for a loaf and took a bite even before taking his seat on the ground. "That food hasn't been blessed," Simeon said.

Logan stopped chewing and dropped the pita on the grass. "Oh, I'm sorry." His family didn't say grace at home or any other prayer for that matter. His stepfather wouldn't hear of it. In fact, the only time he'd ever heard grace said was the few times he'd been a guest for dinner at his friend Franklin's house. Then, and when watching reruns of "The Waltons."

Simeon passed out the loaves to the other shepherds and their sons. He held his own piece with both hands and bowed his head. "Blessed be the Lord our God, Creator of all things seen and unseen, who brings forth this bread from the earth."

After breakfast, Logan and Simeon sat alone on a large outcropping of rocks located near the center of the pasture. They were surrounded by hundreds, if not thousands, of sheep. Logan told Simeon about meeting Robert, about his claim of being an angel and how he mysteriously showed up in his room and brought him to this place. He went on to say how Robert had left him, but not before telling him to find the shepherd.

"That's quite a story," Simeon said. "Many of your words are foreign to me, but it sounds like you had quite an adventure. You say the man who escorted you here was named Robert?"

"That's right," Logan said. "Do you know him? He seemed to know you."

"I don't know anyone by that name in Israel."

The boy's eyes widened. "Israel. Are we near Israel?"

"My son, indeed you are within the boundaries of Israel. We are just outside Bethlehem, the city of David."

"Bethlehem. The place where Jesus was born?"

"I do not know this name, Jesus."

"You live in Israel, but you've never heard of Jesus? Wow, you shepherds are more alone than I thought."

Simeon touched Logan's sleeve. "This thing you

wear over your shirt, what form of garment is it?"

"A jacket."

"And these brass teeth holding the front of it together?" Simeon leaned in close while repeatedly operating the zipper up and down. He smiled in apparent amusement.

"It's called a zipper. Don't you have them here?"

Simeon shook his head. "I wish we did. It looks like a very useful device." He reached down to touch the boy's sneakers. "These things covering your feet are the most unusual sandals I've ever seen."

Although certainly kind enough, Simeon's behavior puzzled Logan. Not knowing who Jesus was, never having seen a jacket, a zipper, or tennis shoes seemed strange, even for a shepherd living out here. And earlier, when he'd been telling him about the homeless man showing up in his apartment, the man looked at him as if he'd been speaking a strange language.

Still, Robert did say the man would help him. But he never said how. Did he mean Simeon would be the one to help Logan find his way home? Robert said he had an errand to run, but he never said how long he'd be gone. Perhaps now was a good time to ask the shepherd for help. Logan's stepfather had told him if he was ever lost in a foreign country to get to the American Embassy there. "Do you know where the American Embassy is in Israel?"

"I'm sorry, but your words mean nothing. What is an emb . . . an embas—"

"An embassy. It's a place where people lost in a foreign country can go for help."

"And the people at this embassy, they will help you get back to your home in, what was it . . . New York?"

"Yes."

"Where in Israel do you think this place would be?"

"It used to be in Tel Aviv, but I think it was moved to Jerusalem last year."

"This first place, I do not know, but Jerusalem I do. It is the holy city of God." Simeon pointed north. "It's about an hour and a half journey in that direction."

"Can you take me there?"

"Yes, but not today. We are still five more days in this pasture before we head north. And we've seen wolves prowling the area. We cannot leave our flocks."

Logan didn't want to wait five days. "I can't wait that long. My parents will be going crazy wondering where I am. Do any of you have a cell phone?"

"I'm afraid I don't know what that is."

"It's a thing you use to call people with." Logan formed his hand around the imaginary shape of a phone and put it up to his ear. "A cell phone."

Simeon scratched the whiskers of his chin and shook his head.

"Don't know what a cell phone is either, huh? Well, then, how about this? Christmas is in four days, and unless I get home by then I'm going to miss it."

"What is this . . . Christmas?"

"You know, December 25th."

Simeon appeared to stare right through him.

"It's a holiday, Jesus's birthday."

"I'm sorry, but I have never heard of it. But if you feel you must leave now, you are welcome to go to Jerusalem on your own."

"Fine. I will." Logan climbed down from the rocks, thrust his hands into his jacket pockets, and stormed off into the pasture.

Once he'd calmed down, Logan thought about making good on his threat to grab his camel and head out by himself. On the other hand, minus a compass or landmarks to lead him, he would probably get lost. And with his luck, he'd no sooner take off than Robert would show up looking for him.

Then there were the wolves.

For the next hour and twenty minutes, Logan walked the pasture while considering his next move. In the distance, he watched Ephraim, Perez, and Asher track down individual or small groups of sheep that had wandered away from the flock. Most times, the boys used a rod or a staff to point the animals back to safety. In the case of a single smaller sheep or lamb, they'd simply lift them onto their shoulders and around their neck to carry them.

Logan turned to the sound of Simeon calling his name. He walked toward Logan across the pasture. Logan pointed to where Asher was guiding two sheep toward the larger group. "Why are they having to keep the sheep together?"

"Sheep are so focused on eating that they don't pay any attention to where they are. A few always eat their way away from the flock. If they wander too far, they'll get lost. Would you like to help round them up?"

Having never been around sheep before, Logan didn't think he'd like the idea of chasing them down. "No, I think I'll pass."

"Then how about this. Have you ever milked sheep where you come from?"

Logan shook his head.

"I'm getting ready to milk some of the ewes.

Would you like to learn how?"

"No, thank you."

"What would you like to do?"

Logan was taken aback by the question. He didn't want to do anything but go home. "Nothing."

"What would you be doing now if you were home?"

"Going to school, watching TV, playing video games."

"These are more words I do not understand. Do they not have work where you come from?"

"Sure they do, but that's mostly for the adults."

"And the children? What work do they do?"

"Some kids I know help with the dishes and keep their room clean. Maybe take out the trash. That's about it."

Simeon covered his mouth with his hand and lowered his eyes. "Hmm."

"But I don't even have to do that."

"I see."

Nearing dusk, Logan and the shepherds gathered where a freshly slaughtered lamb was being cooked over an open fire. Though he'd never eaten lamb before, Logan found the aroma surprisingly appealing. Dinner consisted of the roasted lamb, freshly-curdled cheese, and more unleavened flat bread. As at breakfast, Simeon passed out the loaves of flat bread, to everyone except Logan. After the blessing, Simeon motioned to Zephon seated nearest the roasting lamb. He cut pieces of meat from the lamb, skewed them onto sticks, and passed them to each of the other shepherds, again excluding Logan.

"Excuse me," Logan said. "I think you forgot me."

"We didn't forget you," Simeon said. "Seeing you did no work, we thought you could not possibly be hungry."

Whatever gave him that idea. And whoever said you had to do work in order to be hungry. "Well, I am hungry."

"Do you know the story of the ant?"

Why would I know a story about an ant? "I don't think so. What is it?"

"It's a proverb, one of many from the Book of Proverbs in the Holy Scriptures. It says, 'Go to the ant, you sluggard! Consider her ways and be wise, which, having no captain, overseer or ruler, provides her supplies in the summer, and gathers her food in the harvest.'"

"What's a sluggard?"

"A lazy person who does not work."

Logan's cheeks flushed and his stomach tightened. "Oh, okay. I get it. But couldn't I just have a piece of cheese or some bread to tide me over?"

"Now what would be the lesson in that?"

"It's not fair," Logan heard the whine in his voice. "You can't starve me."

"Starve you." Simeon and the other shepherds chortled. "I doubt one night without food will cause you to waste away."

Eliab was the first to stop laughing. He eyed Logan from behind a smooth, olive face covered by a short, dark beard. "Have you never fasted before?"

"Fasted?" Logan said. "I don't even know what it is."

"It's when you abstain from food for some period of time to honor the Lord."

"Who in their right mind would do that?"

Simeon swept his arm around, gesturing to the other shepherds. "Everyone here."

"Your sons, too?" Logan glanced in succession at Asher, Ephraim, and Perez, each who nodded in response.

"Worry not, my young friend," Simeon said. "Tomorrow, you will have another opportunity to work . . . and likewise, another opportunity to eat."

Perhaps it was just in his head, but the thought of not having anything to eat the rest of the night caused Logan's stomach to rumble, a sensation he hadn't felt since some kid stole his lunch back in first grade. What kind of people were these anyway, withholding food from a kid just because he didn't want to work? Boy, would Robert get an earful when he got back.

CHAPTER 5

December 22

Marcus's passage into the afterlife had been put on hold, at least for now. After leaving his apartment last night, he fully intended to return and complete his business with Messrs, Daniels and Glock. But something about the Ailshie investigation had distracted him. Whether it was the challenge of the mystery on his hands or the urgency of a missing nine-year-old, he didn't know. Now he found himself seated at the head of a large rectangular table in a conference room on the twenty-third floor of the Federal Plaza building.

To his left sat Agents Curtis and Fowlkes. To his right, Special Agent Phillip Lansing, a male with light brown hair in his late twenties.

"Good morning everyone. I hope everyone got a better night's sleep than I did." Marcus stirred two creams and one sugar into his coffee. "So what are we looking at? Murder? Kidnapping, Runaway?"

"Oh, they killed him all right," Phillip said. "No doubt about it."

"The parents?" Todd snorted. "You're that sure?"

"Absolutely," Phillip said. "Who ever heard of a

kid going into his room and never coming out again. A room ten stories off the ground, mind you. And that stunt they pulled with opening the window. Strictly amateur hour. Did they really think anyone was going to buy that ruse?"

Marcus turned to his left. "Janice?"

She slowly tapped the tip of her pen on the table. "I agree with Phillip. I think the boy's probably dead. And since the husband and wife are sticking to the same story, I'd say they're in it together. My theory is the boy never made it to his room last night, and the parents disposed of his body sometime yesterday before they contacted us."

Agent Curtis pulled a report from his binder. "Excuse me. But before anyone starts typing up arrest warrants, I think you're going to want to see the results of the forensic report."

Marcus scooted his chair closer so he could rest his elbows on the table. "Let's hear it."

"As expected, they found Logan's fingerprints and his mother's throughout the bedroom. But they also found another set of adult fingerprints, not the stepfather's. And get this, the unidentified fingerprints were located on the window frame, the sill, and inside the boy's closet. Also recovered from the closet were two, medium-length, dark brown hairs inconsistent with any family member."

The stunned faces of his colleagues told Agent Garraway they were all thinking the same thing.

"I'm not saying they didn't do it," Todd said. "I'm just pointing out there's some other forensic evidence that needs to be accounted for before we go making accusations."

"These unidentified fingerprints—" Marcus said.

Todd nodded. "The lab is running them now. Of course, if they're not in the system, we'll have to wait until we have a suspect in custody to check them against."

"They could be from a maintenance man or other tradesman the Thomases had working in the apartment." Janice said.

"Or from somebody they hired to snatch their kid," Phillip said.

"What are we getting from the PD?" Marcus said.

"Last night they assigned half a dozen officers to help us canvas door-to-door every apartment in the building," Todd said. "They didn't finish until almost two-thirty a.m. In addition, Detective Mahoney advised that every precinct in the five boroughs has the boy's picture and description. Since last night, patrol units have been making periodic checks of all abandoned buildings, arcades, pizzerias, and other youth hangouts. They were also asked to conduct a search of any recognized body-dumping areas located in their respective sectors. The department's Special Victims Division is checking on all known sex offenders and pedophiles residing in the area."

Marcus grabbed his cup, leaned back in his chair, and nodded crisply. "Good. What about the story the mother told us?"

"They located the taxi driver who gave them a ride home. Sure enough, he remembers picking up Logan and his mother on 5th Avenue and dropping them off at their condo a little after three o'clock. The timeline was verified by the doorman, who recalls seeing Mrs. Thomas enter the building with her son at around the same time. Which means if anything happened to the boy, it didn't occur until after he and his mother arrived home."

"Security cameras?"

"The building has four, one in the lobby, two in the garage, and another outside the service entrance in the rear of the building. Other than Mrs. Thomas and Logan entering the lobby at around three, and the husband coming in through the garage at six-thirty, nothing."

Marcus took a sip of coffee "What about motive?"

"What else but money?" Phillip said. "Six to five they've got a big, fat life insurance policy on the boy."

"I don't know, Phillip," Todd said. "The father makes six figures working on Wall Street and they live in one of the swankiest condos on the Upper East Side. From the look of their furnishings, they didn't look like a family hurting for money."

Phillip raised a finger. "Stepfather. And until we know how much debt they're in, I don't care how much money he makes."

Marcus scanned the faces of his team around the table, stopping at Agent Fowlkes.

"You want to polygraph them?" she said.

He took a deep breath and exhaled forcefully. "Not yet. Their son disappeared just yesterday. If there's a chance they're not involved, I don't want to add to their trauma by insinuating we don't believe them. Let's give it a day or two and see what else turns up."

"Like maybe the boy's body?" Phillip said.

"Gosh, I hope not. Let's assume the argument with his mother was more than she made it out to be, and the boy managed to slip out of the apartment without being seen. In the meantime, Todd, I want you to identify anyone who worked in the Thomas apartment in the last six months. Phil, I'll give you a chance to hedge your bet. See if the parents have a life insurance policy on the boy. And Janice, I'd like you to look into the family's finances. Find out if they're in any trouble."

After the room cleared, Marcus walked to a window overlooking the city. Shaking his head, he considered the jumbled expanse of buildings, skyscrapers, parklands and waterways splayed out before him. Finding a needle in a haystack would be child's play compared to locating one small boy in a city of eight million people. And as he'd come to learn in investigating dozens of similar cases, the longer the boy was gone, the less the chances were of his being found alive.

* * *

That evening, twenty-three-year-old Wendell Schlump sat in the front row of chairs, as close as he could get to the speaker's podium, for a gathering of the Manhattan Atheists Association. A skinny kid from the Bronx with oily hair and bad skin, Wendell lived alone in a cheap studio apartment just down the street. Except for his computer and a fascination with atheist philosophy, he had very few outside interests. In fact, this meeting was the highlight of his month, and one of the few social activities he participated in, including any with women. For those, he preferred the services of a prostitute.

The meeting, held monthly in a small basement conference room in Chelsea, routinely drew a crowd of between fifteen to twenty members. But tonight, with Christmas just two days away, attendance was closer to thirty. Included in that membership were a pair of doctors, three lawyers, several stockbrokers, and an Amtrak train engineer. They even had a secretary, Vivian Scofield, who worked for the FBI. Posters lined the walls from the American Atheists, the Freedom from Religion Foundation, and the American Humanist Association, many of which Wendell had used to decorate his own apartment.

Terrance Fishburn, a stout man in his fifties and president of the local chapter, walked to the lectern to the sound of enthusiastic applause. He carried a clipboard. He welcomed the members and opened the meeting by reading from a set of notes, citing the nearly nine percent decrease in the 2019 United States Christian population compared to 2016. He also highlighted the rise to twenty-six percent of those who identified as "no religion" or "unaffiliated" over the same time period. Both statistics received verbal affirmation from the attendees. Mr. Fishburn went on to cite the startling number of church closings affecting the Catholic, Evangelical Lutheran, United Methodist, and Presbyterian churches, and the decrease in infant baptisms.

While these statistics drew some additional response from the assembly, to Wendell they represented affirmation for a position he'd spent years arguing with his parents. Despite their attempts to force a Christian education down his throat by pushing him into Sunday School as a child, by age eleven he'd decided he'd had enough. Tired of the guilt associated with being called a sinner, he began to investigate all sorts of alternative doctrines, including Scientology, Raelism, and the Creativity Movement. Eventually, he moved on to unadulterated Atheism. Boy, would he love to send a copy of Mr. Fishburn's figures to his parents.

Wendell went nuts — standing, cheering, and waving his arms as if he'd won the lottery. Two women on either side of him looked at him with narrowed eyes. A middle-aged man behind them asked him to sit.

Once the crowd quieted, Mr. Fishburn announced they'd received a considerable donation from a private donor. He said the money would be used to mount an ad hoc advertising campaign using the city's bus transit system to cover the final two weeks of the year. He reached behind the podium and produced a red, green, and white sign about thirty-six inches wide by eighteen inches high. On it was an edited version of the popular Christian slogan, Keep Christ in Christmas. Only this sign had an X drawn through the word "in" and the words "OUT OF" printed in large block letters above it.

Laughter broke out when the group saw the sign, followed by more cheering and applause. Again, Wendell couldn't contain himself. He laughed uncontrollably, pointing at the sign and slapping himself on the knee. This time, the two women sitting on either side of him got up and moved several seats away.

Mr. Fishburn raised a hand to quiet the crowd. "Ladies and gentlemen, I ask forgiveness in advance for having to prevail upon you with this last minute request. But as last month's meeting was cancelled and there are just two days remaining before the holiday, I had no alternative. We need as many volunteers as possible to help mount a promotional blitzkrieg to run in conjunction with the transit system campaign. We will be looking for people to man telephone lines, distribute pamphlets on cars at multiple shopping venues, and to man picket locations at several area churches on Christmas Eve. Included in the list of picket sites is a live nativity scene being held in front of First Baptist Church on W 79th Street."

Mr. Fishburn reached into his jacket pocket for a pen and retrieved the clipboard, which Wendell had observed at previous meetings contained a listing of the organization's complete membership. "Can I get a show of hands of anyone willing to work the phones?"

Wendell's hand shot up. Mr Fishburn called out by name all the people who'd raised their hands, thanking each and making entries on the clipboard. He did the same when asking for volunteers to distribute pamphlets and man picket sites. Wendell was the only one who Fishburn thanked all three times.

Following the last query, Wendell raised his hand again. "Mr. Fishburn. I'd like to be assigned to work the live nativity scene."

"Seeing that you're always the first to volunteer for any task required to support this organization's mission, I don't see how I could say no. Thank you."

Though pleased to have been chosen to serve in all three capacities, Wendell wanted to do more than carry a sign or pass out literature. More than just destroy or deface nativity scenes and other symbols of Christianity, which he'd done several times in the past. He hoped to do something really big one day, to make a splash within the atheist community. Something to make people remember him.

CHAPTER 6

December 23

The next morning, Logan bent next to Simeon, who was sitting on a three-legged wooden stool milking a sheep into a clay pot. He'd never heard of sheep being milked, just cows and goats.

"Would you like to give it a try?" Simeon said.

Logan wrinkled his nose and leaned back. "I don't think so."

"Come on. She won't bite. Just take hold of the udder like this." Simeon showed him the grip used for milking.

Logan reached for the other teat but quickly jerked his hand away. "Ooh. It's all mushy."

"Yes, it is. You wouldn't want to try squeezing milk from a rock would you?"

Logan grabbed the teat again and gave a squeeze, but only a couple of drops fell into the pot.

"Pull down slightly on the breast while squeezing." He demonstrated the proper technique again.

On Logan's fourth squeeze he achieved a full squirt. "Hey, I did it."

"We may make a shepherd of you yet." Logan's effort to reach the ewe's udder had pulled the sleeve to his jacket up, exposing his wristwatch. "What's that on your wrist?"

"My watch." He held his arm out for Simeon. "Don't you have watches here either?"

"What is it for?"

"To tell time. How do you know what time it is without a watch?"

"In our villages and around many of our homes we have sundials. But out here in the fields, we rely on the sun during the day and the moon and stars at night to tell us the time."

Golly. These men really were living in the stone ages. Logan had seen a sundial before, but only as part of a History Channel special on ancient civilizations. "What time would you say it is now?"

Simeon looked to the western sky. "About the ninth hour."

"The ninth hour. What is that?"

"The first hour is when the sun comes up." Simeon lifted his wrinkled face to the sky, the cloth on his head parting to reveal a few dark streaks in his hair. "The sixth hour, or noon, is when the sun is at its highest point in the sky. And the twelfth hour is when the sun is going down."

The ninth hour. That would be three hours after noon. Logan looked at his watch. Eight thirty-seven a.m. No way it's that early. The sun was far too low in the west. *Wait a minute, the time zone.* He remembered from watching the news one night that Jerusalem was seven or eight hours ahead of New York. He did the calculations in his head, then nodded. Simeon's guess was pretty close. Not knowing how long he'd be stuck in this time zone, Logan set his watch seven hours ahead.

Simeon and Logan turned to a sound like thunder coming from a dirt road about a hundred yards away. Dozens of men on horseback, dressed in ancient Roman uniforms complete with helmet and body armor, rode in twos along the road.

"Look at that." Logan pointed. "Is somebody making a movie?"

"I do not know this word, movie. Those are Herod's soldiers, heading for Jerusalem."

"Soldiers? Dressed like that? Who is Herod?"

"The King of Judea. A brutal, merciless tyrant who has oppressed his own people."

Logan stared at the soldiers until they disappeared out of sight, dust from the road hanging in the air. "And where is this Judea?"

Simeon swept his arm in an arc in front of them. "All this you see is Judea. Bethlehem, Jerusalem, Jericho, Hebron—they all fall under Herod's rule."

"And how does he oppress them?"

"Many ways, but mostly by levying excessive taxes."

Logan had lost count of the times he'd heard his stepfather and mother complaining about the high taxes associated with living in the city. "Yeah, they do the same to us where I come from."

"One day, Messiah will come and put an end to all oppression."

"Messiah? Isn't that Jesus?"

"I told you, I know not this name. Nevertheless, the prophets have said Messiah would come . . ." Simeon raised a finger. "Wait here." He walked to where his burgundy robe lay on the ground, reached into a leather pouch tucked inside, and returned with a scroll of parchment.

"What's that?"

"Scripture, from the prophet Micah." Simeon opened the scroll and read. "But you, Bethlehem Ephrathah, though you are little among the thousands of Judah, yet out of you shall come forth to Me the One to be Ruler in Israel, whose goings forth are from of old, from everlasting."

"And the One to be Ruler, is this the Messiah?"

"Yes. It is why I chose to live in Bethlehem. So that if He should come during my lifetime, I might be here to bear witness to it."

"I hate to have to tell you this, but he already came. A little over two thousand years ago."

Simeon chuckled. "That cannot be. Two thousand years ago was before David, before Moses, before our father, Abraham. Scripture tells us the Messiah will descend from the line of David."

Simeon didn't make sense. Those guys—David, Moses, and Abraham, had all come before Jesus, right? Logan had heard their names in Sunday school. But the timing didn't work. If they lived less than two thousand years before, then that meant they came after Jesus. And Logan knew that wasn't right.

He was so confused.

And why did this guy keep talking like Jesus hasn't come yet? Could he be like some of the Jewish kids back home who didn't celebrate Christmas? "But that's what I was trying to tell you yesterday. Jesus was born on Christmas day."

"Again, your words are strange to me. But I assure you, Messiah hasn't come yet. Otherwise, Herod would have been deposed long ago."

Logan couldn't remember exactly the name of the current leader of Israel, but he was pretty sure it wasn't Herod. His recollection of news events was the leader was someone whose name started with the letter N—something "yahoo," but he wasn't sure. Either way, he didn't want to risk offending the man who'd helped him by continuing to argue the point. Barring Robert's return beforehand, Logan would be at the embassy in Jerusalem in a few days at worst, a guest of *whoever* was in charge of the country.

* * *

Shortly after 8 p.m., Simeon and Logan made their beds out of woolen blankets next to each other under a small tree on a hill in the pasture. The other shepherds and their sons bedded down nearby. A repeat of last night's moon lit the rolling hills dotted with sheep. Logan lay with his hands folded behind his head and gazed at the stars, the reflection of a small campfire flickering off the blankets. "You know, where I come from I never see stars like this."

"The stars don't shine in New York City?"

"They do. But the city is so filled with lights that I hardly ever notice the ones in the sky."

"Ah, I see. Jerusalem is the same. There are so many lanterns burning throughout the city at night, the stars are diminished by them."

Logan took in the majestic sight. "I've never seen anything so beautiful."

"Yes, it's—"

A noise cut off Simeon's words. They turned to the sound of a disturbance off to their left. A large group of sheep, bleating nervously, moved toward them, followed by the low bellow of a ram's horn being blown by another shepherd.

"Wolf!" someone cried from farther down the hill.

Simeon and Logan jumped up. "Stay here," Simeon said, grabbing his crook and a smaller leather pouch before charging down the hill.

Logan stood clutching the trunk of the tree while peering at the confrontation unfolding in the darkness below. Jachin and Eliab called for Simeon and Zephon to join them somewhere down the hill to the left of the tree. Dozens of sheep were being scattered along the edge of the herd there. He peered through the darkness and caught sight of the problem. From here, they looked like a pack of dogs, but then he recalled Simeon's warning about the wolves. He counted six of them.

While he'd been distracted, part of the flock had moved in his direction. Before he realized it, he found himself surrounded and pinned up against the tree by dozens of frantic sheep. He couldn't get away and shook uncontrollably. He was going to get trampled!

He pushed his way among the animals and away from the tree. When he finally got past the wooly, stinky crowd, he followed the path Simeon had taken down the hill and toward the area where the sheep were scattered.

He found two dead sheep and a dead wolf and shuddered at the sight of the bodies.

"Simeon," a shepherd called in the distance. When Simeon didn't answer, the man called again.

Simeon said nothing.

A deep, menacing growl caused Logan to wheel around. A snarling wolf stood twenty feet away licking his fangs.

Logan tried to cry out, but no sound exited his mouth. He wanted to run, but his feet froze to the ground.

The wolf stalked toward him.

Somehow, Logan coaxed his feet to move and backed away, only its stride was longer than his. The wolf crept closer. It lowered its head and raised its haunches. The animal was going to pounce!

Logan raced in the only direction open to him, away from where he'd last seen the shepherds. Behind him, the sound of the wolf's pounding paws and angry snarls told him the animal was gaining ground. Logan tried turning back up the hill into the sheep herd to gain some cover, only the wolf had positioned itself between them.

Logan bolted into the open field.

He tried running faster, but the sounds made by the pursuing wolf only seemed to be getting closer. He felt a tug on his pants' leg. The wolf tore off a mouthful of cloth, and Logan stumbled but kept running.

A few seconds later, a pair of paws crashed against his back between the shoulder blades, driving him to the ground.

The wolf bit into his right shoulder.

Logan screamed.

CHAPTER 7

Just after lunch, Marcus had just opened a folder on his desk when Agent Lansing entered his office, a gleam in his eye and an open notepad in his hand. So anxious was he to reach his supervisor's desk, he completely ignored Janice seated in a chair just inside the doorway. "Find something?" Marcus said.

"Bingo," Phil said. "The Thomases have three policies with New York Life. A million each on the husband and wife, five hundred thou' on the boy."

"A half a million in New York City?" Janice said. "In this economy? Not exactly a fortune."

"Hey, five hundred thousand is five hundred thousand . . . in any economy."

"The husband makes almost twice that in a year," Janice said, "a little over nine hundred K. You think he'd risk life in prison for six months' pay? It hardly seems worth it."

"Parents better off than them have gotten rid of their kids for less. What kind of debt are they in?"

"I'm still running down a few things, but I did get responses back from the credit bureaus. And what I can tell you is their credit is just below the excellent range, seven-eighty-two. I doubt they're having trouble paying their bills."

"I still say they could have done it for the money," Phil said." Let's watch and see how long it takes them to put in a claim. That'll be the clincher."

Marcus looked at the documents in the folder in front of him. "Phil, before you came in, we were discussing these three reports that Janice handed me. I think you'll find them interesting. The first two are forensic reports from our Latent Print Unit and our Trace Evidence Unit, respectively. The third is from the National Personnel Records Center."

Phil slowly backed away from the desk and took a seat next to Janice.

"The unidentified fingerprints found in the boy's bedroom belong to a man named Robert Ford Templeton. He was a private in the United States Army who served with the 4th Infantry Division during World War II."

"World War II? You're kidding, right?" Phil looked up, as though deep in thought. "Let's see, that's . . . even if he was only eighteen at the time, that would make him over ninety-years-old. Are you saying we've got some ninety-year-old geezer out there snatching kids from their apartments?"

Marcus shook his head. "I would if he were still alive. But he died on June 6, 1944 at Utah Beach during the allied landing at Normandy.

"What!"

Marcus turned the page of the third document. "Listen to this. Shortly after landing on the beach, Private Templeton and his platoon were pinned down by overlapping fields of machine-gun fire coming from two nearby German fortifications. Despite this murderous crossfire, witnesses testified Templeton single-handedly charged one of the bunkers and tossed in two grenades, killing everyone inside. He then joined his fellow soldiers in an assault on the second emplacement before being cut down by enemy fire. Private Templeton was credited with saving the lives of over thirty members of his platoon. He was awarded the Medal of Honor—posthumously, of course."

"Whoa, wait a minute here," Phil said. "Now you're starting to scare me. Are you telling me the prints in that apartment belong to a man who's been dead for seventy-six years?"

"It's been triple-checked."

"Well, then, you'd better have them check it again. Because what you just described isn't possible."

"Yeah, I know."

Janice leaned forward in her chair. "What about the trace evidence report? Anything useful there?"

"Neither of the two hairs they recovered had the follicle attached, which means the lab is having to try to isolate mitochondrial DNA," Marcus said. "Unfortunately, it's going to take a little longer to get back those results."

"So, what are we going to do in the meantime?" Janice said.

Marcus slammed the folder shut. "For now, we're going to continue with our investigation as if this evidence doesn't exist. Let's not forget, our primary goal is to recover Logan alive. And I don't want the existence of some questionable piece of evidence to distract from that objective. Let's just follow the leads we have and hope this turns out to be one colossal mistake."

Since taking over as the supervisor of the Northeast Region's CARD Team, Marcus had overseen dozens of child abduction cases, many involved unusual, or even gruesome, circumstances. But never anything like this. A boy mysteriously disappears from his bedroom in a tenth-floor apartment, and the only physical evidence available points to a dead war hero from the previous century. This case was starting to sound like an episode of the *Twilight Zone*. Part of him was hoping they wouldn't be able to obtain any DNA from the hair strands. He wasn't too keen on the idea of having to go to Arlington National Cemetery to dig up Private Templeton to do the comparison.

* * *

A loud thump sounded against the wolf's body, causing it to let out a yelp and release its bite on Logan.

Two more thumps followed, along with two more yelps, and the wolf rolled off his back onto the ground, writhing in pain. Three stones about the size of Logan's fist lay at the animal's side.

Simeon, accompanied by Eliab and Jachin, ran up with his crook and bashed the wolf's skull in. Each shepherd held a sling.

Simeon knelt and gently turned Logan over, who hugged the man, crying uncontrollably. "It is all right now." Simeon patted his back. "The wolf is dead."

"You saved my life." He hugged Simeon harder.

The shepherd removed Logan's jacket and shirt to examine the wound. "Hmm. No doubt painful, but not serious. I thought I told you to stay by the tree?"

"I know." He gestured up the hill to the crowd of sheep surrounding it. "But all those sheep were about to squish me."

In the dim moonlight, Logan saw Simeon's eyebrows lift. "I see. A far better fate than being eaten by a wolf though, don't you think?"

His companions joined him in a laugh.

Logan agreed but he didn't feel like laughing. "Where are Zephon and the boys?"

"Chasing down the other wolves," Simeon said.

Logan pointed to the small piece of leather with strings of cord attached to either end in his hand. "Is that a sling?"

"Indeed. Have you never seen one before?"

"Only on TV. Isn't that how David killed Goliath?"

"I don't know TV, but yes, it is what King David used to slay the giant."

"My mother taught me about it, but my stepfather says it's just a fairytale. He says everything in the Bible is a fairytale."

"And what is a fairytale?"

Simeon's lack of understanding of common terms continued to mystify Logan. How could he not know what a cell phone, TV, or fairytale was? Was it the difference in cultures? Or could it simply be the result of the life of a shepherd living alone in the fields? "My stepfather said it's a story told to teach a lesson but not really true."

"Let me assure you, my son, the story of David and Goliath *is* true. It was written by one of Israel's greatest leaders, the prophet Samuel."

This was the second time since Logan's arrival Simeon had addressed him as "son," a term his stepfather had never used in the six years he'd known him. "I don't think I remember my mother telling me about him." Even with his shoulder pounding, Logan couldn't keep his eyes off the sling in Simeon's hand.

"Would you like to hold it?"

"Can I?"

Simeon handed him the weapon.

"And this is what you used to throw those rocks?"

"A simple weapon but hard to master."

"Could you teach me how to use it?"

The shepherd nodded. "Perhaps when you are feeling better. But right now we need to get some fire on your wound to purify it and stop the bleeding."

Logan's head snapped back. "Fire?"

Simeon helped the boy back to their campsite, retrieved a small stick, then skinned the bark with a knife.

"What's that for?" the boy said.

"For you to bite on. This is going to hurt."

Logan drew back. "Can't you just put on some antiseptic and a Band-Aid?"

"I don't know what those are, but out here this is the best we can do. Be thankful the flesh doesn't require sewing."

Simeon placed the stick in the boy's mouth and grabbed him firmly by both elbows. He motioned to Jachin, who pulled a branch with a smoldering end from the fire and laid it against the wound.

His flesh burned, and Logan let out a high-pitched scream, digging his fingernails into Simeon's forearms before falling against his chest in tears.

"The worst is over." Simeon lifted the boy's chin and removed the stick. "As soon as it dries, we will put some salve on the wound to promote healing."

Dumbfounded the shepherds had actually used a burning stick to treat his wolf bite, Logan couldn't wait to get home. He vowed never to complain again to his mother about having to go to a doctor. On the other hand, was he ever glad he chose not to take off for Jerusalem by himself. The wolves would have gotten him for sure.

A half hour later, Logan struggled to get comfortable in his makeshift bed, his shoulder throbbing to the beat of his heart.

"You had best try sleeping on your opposite side or on your stomach," Simeon said. "That is, if you can still sleep after all this excitement."

Zephon appeared out of the darkness to join them.

"Aren't you coming to bed?" Logan said.

Simeon looked to his companion, who shook his head. Simeon turned back to Logan. "Not tonight. Four of those wolves escaped, so we'll have to stand guard until daylight."

Logan lay on his opposite shoulder, one eye open to watch Simeon, who stood only a few feet away leaning on his crook. But Logan grew tired despite the pain. He fell asleep thinking about all those presents waiting for him at home under the tree. *Can't wait to open my new iPhone.*

CHAPTER 8

December 24

The next morning, Marcus drove slowly along a winding cemetery path, past the hundreds of gravestones littering the grounds on either side of the roadway. Wreaths and poinsettias adorned many of the markers, a few others, a Menorah. But the FBI supervisor had no intention of entertaining a similar ritual. No twisted ring of pine or fir branches to garnish his wife's headstone, no red-leafed plant in a cheap foil-covered pot to mark her place of rest. For him, Christmas wasn't something to celebrate, or even to commemorate. Just another day of mourning, a stark reminder of the nightmare from which he'd never wake up.

He slowed to make a left turn onto a path running parallel to a line of trees near the back of the cemetery. Driving another thirty yards, he stopped the car and made his way to a line of grave sites next to the wood line. He paused in front of one cross-shaped headstone.

Carolyn Louise Garraway
Beloved Wife
April 16, 1979 – December 24, 2018

"I'm here, Darling," he said, his throat tightening. "It's time." This was the day he'd always planned to end his life, on the anniversary of his wife's death. And what better place to leave this world than at Carolyn's graveside. They could just dig a hole next to her and roll him into it. No coffin necessary. Just leave him for the worms. But his state of inebriation four nights ago had interrupted his timetable, tempting him to start the party early.

Nothing to impair his judgment now.

Marcus reached to his waist and wrapped his hand around the butt of his gun, placing his thumb on the holster snap.

He hesitated, then dropped to his knees with tears welling his eyes. "Oh, Carolyn, I miss you so much. Especially today." He removed his hand from the weapon to wipe his eyes. "I just wanted to tell you how sorry I am and hope you can forgive me." He leaned against the cross. "I know. I should have gone with you to Albany, especially when I knew there was a possibility of snow that weekend. But we'd just apprehended the man who'd kidnapped the little Taylor girl, and I wanted to be there for the interrogation." Marcus wiped his nose on his sleeve. "Even though I didn't have to be. Janice and Todd had it under control. I should have trusted them. But I was selfish and determined to stay."

Marcus grasped his gun, but the sound of footsteps on the pathway behind him diverted his attention. He rose to his feet and turned toward the distraction. A young man in his thirties wearing a green army jacket approached. A small red ball hung from a buttonhole in his coat and swung back and forth. The man left the path to cross the grassy area between them, then stopped a few yards from Carolyn's marker. *Oh great. Some bum looking for money.* "What do you want?" Marcus said.

The man raised his hands chest high. "I'm no threat, mister."

"What do you mean?"

The stranger pointed to where the agent's hand rested on his weapon.

Marcus jerked his hand away. "Oh, I'm sorry. Just instinct, I guess. But you needn't be concerned about the weapon. I'm with the FBI."

"I'm glad to hear that."

"What can I do for you?" Here it comes. *Do you have any spare change? I haven't eaten in two days. My car ran out of gas, could you spare a couple of bucks? We just got evicted and my baby needs formula or diapers.*

"Actually, I stopped to see if there was anything I could do for *you*. I saw you leaning against the headstone and thought you might be ill or injured."

"No, I'm all right. But thank you for your concern."

The man pointed to the headstone. "Someone close to you?"

"My wife."

"I'm sorry." The man leaned forward while squinting, as though closely examining the marker. "I see she died on this day. Now I'm doubly sorry."

"Thanks, but you needn't be. Christmas doesn't hold any special meaning for me."

The man placed a finger to his lips. "Hmm. You mind if I ask if you felt that way before your wife died?"

Why's this guy so interested in my personal life? Probably time for a gracious exit. On the other hand, the man did stop to check on Marcus's welfare. "No.

But even then it was my wife's love of Christmas that made it something special, as opposed to any personal religious conviction."

"I see. You didn't really believe in the true meaning of Christmas before your wife passed away?"

Uh, oh. Not just a bum. A Bible-thumper. "If you're talking about a virgin giving birth to the Son of God, no, I don't believe it. Although my wife was continually making the case for it."

"It sounds like your wife was a very insightful woman."

Yep. A Bible-thumper. Why do I always attract the crazies? "Just because she believed in Jesus?"

"That's certainly one reason, but—" The man paused and looked at the gun on Marcus's hip. "Hey, you weren't thinking of doing something rash before I came up, were you?"

Marcus blinked to clear the tears. "What gave you that idea?"

"Oh, I don't know." The man tipped his finger toward him. "The red eyes. Today being the anniversary of your wife's death. You having your hand on your gun when I walked up."

"And if I did, what business is it of yours?"

"The sanctity of life is everyone's business, my friend. Stop and think for a minute. And try . . . just for a moment . . . to put aside your own pain. Do you really think your wife would want you to consider suicide?"

Like a tidal wave, memories of Carolyn rushed in. The loving way she looked at him every day he stepped through the door from work. The softness of her touch whenever she held his hand. The soothing, gentleness in her voice each time she told him she loved him. Never perfunctory, or out of some sense of obligation, but with absolute sincerity of heart. And to think it took some poor homeless guy to point it out.

Marcus dropped his head and sobbed. "No, she wouldn't."

"Besides, aren't you in the middle of an important investigation into a boy's disappearance?"

Marcus lifted his head, his moist eyes widening. First, it's my state of mind, now it's the investigation. How does this guy know these things? "As a matter of fact, I am. But I don't see how you could possibly know anything about me or the case."

"I may look like I can't afford a newspaper, but I do still get to read one on occasion."

Marcus didn't remember his name being mentioned in the media, or how this guy would know who he was. Still, the man had stopped him from making a tragic mistake. For now. He should acknowledge it. "I want to thank you for coming by when you did and for pointing out something that should have been obvious to me."

"Completely understandable. Pain has a way of clouding everyone's judgment at one time or another. The thing to remember is over time, even our worst pains tend to subside."

For a guy who looked like he'd just come from skid row, he had a remarkable grasp of psychology and human nature. "I'll try to keep that in mind. Anything else?"

"As a matter of fact, yes. Honor your wife by cherishing your own life. Keep your gun in its holster. Go easy on the Jack. Most importantly, embrace your civic responsibilities. There's a nine-year-old boy out there who needs your help. And now, you need his."

Marcus faced Carolyn's headstone, leaned over, and kissed the top of it. "Goodbye, Darling," he whispered. "I'll be back, thanks to mister . . . mister — "

Realizing he hadn't bothered to ask the homeless man his name, Marcus turned and extended his arm in anticipation of introducing himself and shaking the man's hand.

But he'd vanished.

Marcus scanned the cemetery, then walked to his car and scanned it again. Nothing but rows and rows of headstones. No way the man could have made it out of sight in the few moments Marcus had his back turned. And why hadn't he heard the man's footsteps on the path walking away the way he had when he first arrived? The man had disappeared, literally.

Marcus climbed into his car and started the ignition.

Wait a minute. How did he know about Jack?

* * *

Logan had been helping Asher and Perez round up strays on a hill before the sun set when his attention was drawn to movement on the road below. A man leading a donkey with a woman riding on its back approached along the same dirt highway used yesterday by the soldiers. As they drew near, the couple veered from the road and crossed the pasture toward the flocks.

"Someone's coming," Logan called to Simeon.

He walked down the hill and stood beside Logan as the couple reached the edge of the encampment.

"Greetings," the man said. "We've traveled far.

Might I trouble you for a cup of milk for my wife?"

Not only was it obvious the woman was pregnant, but there was something familiar about the couple Logan couldn't quite put his finger on. Or the reason for the funny feeling welling in his stomach.

"Logan, would you bring one of the pots we filled today and a cup for each of our guests?" Simeon gestured toward their campfire. "Please, come and warm yourselves."

Despite his sore shoulder, Logan hurried down the hill and returned a minute later, sloshing milk as he ran.

Simeon raised a hand. "Slow down, son, lest there be none left for them to drink."

Logan walked the last few yards and handed the milk to the couple seated by the fire. The man reached into his tunic and handed him a small copper coin.

"Gee, thanks." The boy studied the strange coin for a moment before putting it into the pocket of his jeans. Logan caught the woman looking him over between sips of milk.

"You're a stranger in this land," she said.

"How did you know?"

"You dress oddly for a shepherd boy."

"The boy is a visitor from the west." Simeon grabbed the pot and poured more milk into each of their cups. "Would you care for something to eat?"

The man looked to his wife, who, after touching her stomach, offered a slight shake of her head. "No, thank you," he said." The milk is excellent."

"You say you've traveled far?"

"From Nazareth," the man said.

"That *is* quite a journey," Simeon said. "Where are you headed?"

"We were hoping to make it to Bethlehem before nightfall."

Simeon nodded. "You will. You are close."

"I know," the man said. "I was born there."

"So was I. Are you traveling for the census?"

The man nodded. "Little else would cause us to travel this far from home with my wife in this condition."

"Unfortunately, the decrees of Augustus make no provision for the timing of childbirth."

"I would see more freedom and less decrees from Rome."

"As would I."

The woman let out a soft gasp. She wore a pained look as she reached for her husband's arm. "The child stirs."

"We should go." The man stood, helped his wife up, and lifted her back onto their animal. He turned to Simeon. "We were fortunate indeed to encounter the shepherds of Israel along the road rather than bandits. Thank you."

"May the Lord bless you for your charity," the woman said.

Still curious as to their identity, Logan followed a short distance behind the couple, stopping at the edge of the pasture while they continued down to the road. Something about the profile of a man leading a woman on a donkey stuck in his mind from his early childhood. *Mary and Joseph. Nah, it couldn't be.* But who would have thought that in the twenty-first century he would have encountered a couple who so closely resembled the parents of Jesus?

Logan turned to head back to camp and depressed the date button on his watch.

Tomorrow was Christmas.

* * *

After leaving the cemetery, Marcus had stopped by the office for a couple of hours to catch up on some paperwork. Now, on the way home, he slowed at the sight of a dozen or more people entering a church on the right side of the street. He turned into the parking lot of Trinity Church and drove past the sign that displayed "Christmas Eve Services, 6:00 p.m. and 8:00 p.m." He parked the car but left the engine running.

Of all the activities associated with celebrating the holiday, going to church on Christmas Eve was Carolyn's favorite. Sure, she enjoyed the host of other traditions, like decorating their home in Staten Island, wrapping gifts, sending cards, baking cookies, or sitting down to watch their favorite Christmas movies. But what really moved her, what she never took for granted, was the opportunity to worship her Lord on this night.

She also used her favorite time to try evangelizing her husband. While she didn't press the issue much the rest of the year, at every Christmas Eve and Easter service she'd lean over and whisper in Marcus's ear, "Good day to get saved."

After a few minutes, cars ceased coming into the parking lot. Marcus thought he heard music emanating from inside the church and lowered the window to hear over the sound of the car's engine. Part of him wanted to go in, the part that'd accompanied Carolyn this night every year of their marriage, and a couple before then. But he just couldn't bring himself to go through with it. Without her, it just wouldn't be the same. When the choir began the first verse of "Joy to the World," the irony became too much for him to take. He rolled up the window, put the car in gear, and drove hastily out of the lot.

For the rest of the ride home, Marcus couldn't stop thinking about his encounter with the mysterious stranger this afternoon. How did the guy know all those things about him and his investigation? And what did he mean by, "And now, you need his?"

Marcus looked forward to having a drink when he got home. Only this time, he'd resolved to take the stranger's advice and secure his weapon in the gun lockbox in his closet before breaking out the Old No.7.

CHAPTER 9

December 25

Logan pulled the scratchy wool blanket over his head to block the bright light that'd disturbed his sleep. He thought he was dreaming — it was way too soon to be morning — until Simeon touched his arm. "Wake up, son."

Logan squinted and pulled the blanket down.

He sat upright at the sight of an unusual light shining on the field around them. And yet, in the background, stars sparkled in the night sky. Zephon, Jachin, and Ephraim gathered to the left of Simeon and trembled. Eliab, along with his two sons, hid behind the tree. Thirty feet away, a man in a long white robe with a gold band circling his chest hovered a few feet above the ground. Logan blinked. How did he do that? The light appeared to be coming *from* him.

"Fear not," the man said, "for behold, I bring you good tidings of great joy, which shall be to all people."

His voice echoed as if spoken through a megaphone. At the same time, it was like the sound of a running brook or stream. Simeon and the other shepherds all bowed to the ground.

Logan did the same, overcome by the man's . . .

brightness, and . . . he didn't know how to describe it. He only knew the light was different and somehow better, more stunning, than anything he'd ever seen.

The man in white said, "For unto you is born this day in the city of David, a Savior, which is Christ the Lord. And this shall be a sign unto you. You shall find the babe wrapped in swaddling clothes, lying in a manger."

Logan had heard those words before, but he couldn't place where.

Simeon and his friends lifted their heads to see thousands of beings appear in the night sky to join the man with the gold band. Each wore a shining white robe, and they encircled the entire area lit by the light from the first man. The scene reminded Logan of a crowded Giants football stadium packed with fans. Only this crowd was much larger, and a whole lot closer than the fans were to the fifty-yard line. Despite the angel's admonishment to not fear, Logan shuddered. His mouth fell open while his eyes peered all around.

Music played, though not from any instrument Logan could identify. More like voices singing notes without words. Logan had never heard anything so beautiful, and the sound gave him chills. Then, the multitude spoke with booming voices. "Glory to God in the highest, And on earth peace, good will toward men." Like the first man, their voices seemed to echo into the darkness.

When they finished, the massive crowd was drawn up into heaven, including the man with the gold band. Once they disappeared, an unusually bright star shone where the strange beings had been.

The shepherds gathered together, hugging one

another and uttering praises to God.

"Who was that?" Logan said.

"Angels." Simeon's eyes sparkled.

"My stepdad says there's no such thing as angels, that they're just another myth from the Bible."

"A myth?"

"You know, a fable, or what I said before, a fairytale."

"Son, I've heard quite a few fables in my lifetime. I've even told a few myself." Simeon pointed up to the place where the angels disappeared. "But I'll tell you this. What we just witnessed is not one of them."

Simeon was right. With all due respect to his stepfather's doubt, Logan had seen something with his own eyes and ears that couldn't be ignored. An experience made all the more puzzling by the fact he recognized the angel's words. Where had he heard them before? *Charlie Brown. That's it!* The angel's words were from a speech made by Linus in *A Charlie Brown Christmas,* a holiday special he'd watched on TV every year since the age of five.

"And I'll tell you something else," Simeon said, "Do you remember what I told you yesterday about the Messiah, about how the prophet Micah predicted His coming forth out of Bethlehem?"

"Sure. You think the angel was talking about the same thing?"

"I think what the angel told us tonight is the fulfillment of Micah's prophecy."

"So what do we do now?" Logan said.

"We go find the Messiah."

Simeon motioned to the other adult shepherds. "Let us now go to Bethlehem and see this thing that has come to pass, which the Lord has made known to us." All nodded in agreement.

"How will we know where to find Him?" Logan said.

"We will look for the sign the angel spoke of," Simeon said. "A babe wrapped in swaddling clothes lying in a manger."

"How does that help us to locate Him?"

"We shall look in barns, pens, and stables, wherever livestock are kept. How many babies will be lying in a feed trough?" Simeon packed a leather pouch with bread, olives, dried fruit, and cheese for the journey. Meanwhile, Jachin, Zephon, and Eliab gave instructions to their sons to safeguard the flock for the remainder of the night while they were gone.

Logan approached the old shepherd. "Simeon."

"What is it, son."

"I have something I need to tell you."

The shepherd paused from packing to give the boy his full attention.

"The words the angel spoke. They were familiar to me."

"What words?"

"All of them. The ones about a Savior being born today in the city of David, and about finding him wrapped in swaddling clothes, lying in a manger. Even the part about there being peace on earth and good will toward men. I've heard them before. They're talking about Jesus, aren't they?"

Simeon nodded. "I think I understand now. This Jesus is the name the people from your country have given to the Messiah."

They must be talking about the same person. Only how could that be? The Jesus he'd heard about had been born over two thousand years before, yet the angel said He was born today. Perhaps their journey into the city would help to solve the mystery. "How far is it to Bethlehem?"

The shepherd motioned to the southern horizon. "Right over that rise. We should be there in less than an hour."

"Hey, I just thought of something," Logan said. "Do you think the Messiah could belong to the couple who passed by here?"

Simeon's smile was wide. "It could very well be, my son."

Logan and the shepherds set out on foot for the city of David.

* * *

Early on Christmas morning, Wendell awoke to the sound of a drunk throwing up in the corner of their holding cell at Central Booking in the Tombs. Combined with the smell of body odor, urine, and unwashed socks, it made for a unique, yet sadly unforgettable, breathing experience. He slowly scanned the enclosure he shared with eighteen men of varying races, social status, and dispositions, many of whom sat, or lay sleeping on the floor. Others, himself included, simply propped themselves up against the cell bars.

A throbbing over his left eye prompted him to reach for his forehead, an impulse he instantly regretted when his fingers touched a lump there. The pain served to initiate a replay of the previous night's activities.

As scheduled, Wendell, another male, and two female members of the Manhattan Atheists showed up to protest the live Nativity Scene in front of the First Baptist Church. Each carried a sign that read "Don't be Fooled, Jesus is a Myth." And despite some cold stares from the company of actors, things remained peaceful for the first thirty minutes. Wendell and his cohorts marched back and forth along the sidewalk in front of the display chanting their slogan but made no effort to hinder visitors.

Four of these visitors, a young couple with two small children, a boy and a girl, stood a few feet away from the front of the display. Wendell had been content to pass behind them when walking his protest route but chose this time to cut in front of them. When he did, the bottom of his picket sign accidently struck the young boy on the side of the head, causing him to cry out. The father approached Wendell and grabbed hold of the picket handle. "What do you think you're doing?"

"I'm sorry sir, I didn't mean to hurt the boy," Wendell said.

"You didn't mean to? You deliberately walked right in front of us."

"It was an accident."

This seemed to mollify the father a bit, who released his grip on the sign. But the two were soon joined by the man playing the Joseph character in the Nativity. "It's Christmas Eve," Joseph said. "Why don't you God-haters go somewhere else to peddle your poison?"

Wendell jutted out his chin. "Our poison, as you say, is protected by the Constitution, and the separation of church and state."

"Oh yeah?" Joseph ripped the sign away from Wendell and broke it over his knee before tossing it on the ground. "Separate that."

Wendell clenched his fists and felt heat rising up his neck. He cursed and charged the man. The two threw punches and wrestled toward the stable. As they drew near, the Mary character pulled the live infant from the manger moments before the two stumbled over it, breaking it in pieces. They continued to wrestle and exchange blows, crashing into the back of the stable and bringing the whole structure down on top of them.

A few minutes later, the police arrived and after interviewing a half dozen witnesses, arrested Wendell for assault. He was booked at the local precinct and transported to the Tombs overnight to await arraignment.

"All right, gentlemen," a guard from the jail said while turning a key in the cell door lock. "We're taking you up for arraignment. Stand and line up against the bars single file." Several guards entered the cell block and shackled the men together in groups of six. Each of the groups, including the one Wendell found himself chained to, was transported to the courthouse in a white Department of Corrections bus. When his case was called, he pled not guilty. The judge set bail in the amount of five-hundred dollars, an amount Wendell obtained via a bond posted by a bail bondsman for the customary ten percent fee.

Two hours later, Wendell descended the steps of the courthouse in triumph, proud to have spent Christmas in jail, and in the process, strike his first blow, literally, for the cause. His only regret — the fear his arrest would jeopardize his chances of getting the new job he'd applied for to work as a janitor.

CHAPTER 10

Dawn was still a few hours away when Logan and the shepherds entered Bethlehem. Instead of a modern town with paved streets and contemporary buildings, the travelers walked on dirt roads lined by flat roof houses made of chiseled stone. And there wasn't a car or truck anywhere.

The streets were nearly deserted, except for an occasional drunk staggering down the block or curled up in a doorway and a few women who wore too much makeup. The latter made several attempts to engage the shepherds, all without success. But Simeon used the opportunity to inquire of the women if they'd seen or heard of any expectant woman who'd recently entered the city. One of them suggested we check at one of the four inns, although only two might still be open. He paid the woman a strange looking coin for the information.

Simeon knew the inns, the first was only a few streets away. He said checking the inns would be a good strategy because most included a place for travelers to board their horses or donkeys.

It took several minutes of pounding on the door of the first inn before an angry voice on the other side turned Logan and the shepherds away. Through the closed door, the proprietor denied having any vacancies or seeing a woman heavy with child. He followed this with a threat to do bodily harm to the travelers if they didn't leave immediately. Before leaving, Simeon checked a small fenced-in area on the right side of the inn where a half a dozen donkeys rested. The only manger they saw was filled with hay.

On the other side of the town, down several long streets, stood the second inn. Fortunately, the innkeeper, a balding fat man with a full dark beard and wearing a beige tunic, flung open the door on the third knock and invited them inside.

"I don't have any room, but you can spend the remainder of the night in my rear stable. There's a young couple already there, as long as you don't mind sharing."

Simeon's eyes brightened. "Thank you. We accept your offer."

He gave the innkeeper a few coins and led Logan and the other shepherds to the rear of the inn.

An open-walled stable had been cut into a large outcropping of rock. Several lanterns burned along the back and side walls of the structure. A cow, two donkeys, two goats, and a few sheep lay on the floor. Beneath one of the lanterns on the back wall sat the man and woman who'd visited their camp earlier that day. They huddled together overlooking a manger filled with straw. On top of the straw lay a newborn baby wrapped in rags.

Simeon and the shepherds approached the manger and bowed to the ground. Logan stood a few feet behind them, eyes wide, heart pounding. How was this happening? Logan had seen enough pictures, carvings, and models of the Nativity to recognize the scene before him. This was either the actual birth of Jesus, or somebody was putting on a pretty good show. Considering the angels, he had to believe his eyes and ears.

Simeon used his staff to pull himself up to a kneeling position next to the manger. He raised his hand toward the child, pausing midway to look at the woman.

She nodded.

He gently touched the baby on the top of the head. Tears streamed down his cheek. "Messiah," he whispered.

"What brings you shepherds here at this time of night?" the man said.

"An angel appeared to us in the fields and told us of the birth of the Christ child. We are here to worship him. But we do not know his name."

"His name is Jesus."

"Jesus," Simeon repeated. He and the other shepherds stared at Logan.

"I am Joseph." The man motioned toward the woman. "This is my wife—"

"Mary," Logan said.

A hand flew to the woman's chest, her lips parted. "Logan, is it?"

"Yes, ma'am."

"The God of Abraham has blessed you with quite a gift, this ability to see names. Who are you?"

"He is a prophet from another country," Simeon said. "One who not only knew your names but the name of the child before he was born. Logan also foresaw the message declared by the angel tonight before he spoke it."

Mary smiled at him. "A prophet indeed."

Logan couldn't ignore the obvious any longer. What he'd first assumed was simply a clash of cultures had suddenly taken on supernatural significance. Simeon's ignorance of modern-day conventions, clothing, time-keeping, and Tel-Aviv, the second-most recognizable city in Israel, had nothing to do with the place they were in. It had to do with the time. Somehow, Logan had been swept back in history to the period of Jesus's birth. "Begging your pardon, ma'am, but I'm not a prophet. I'm from the future."

"The future?" Her eyebrows lifted, and she glanced at Joseph before focusing on him again. "How can someone be from somewhere before its time?"

Logan scratched his head. He hadn't a clue how to explain it, and even if he did, he doubted they would understand or believe him. He considered telling her what he knew about Jesus's fate, of how he would eventually be crucified, but decided against it. He couldn't bring himself to ruin the joy of the moment with a prediction of the baby's death. Instead he moved toward the manger. "May I?"

Mary nodded again.

Logan stood next to the manger, resting his hands on one of the top slats of the trough. He'd seen plenty of babies in his time, but none quite like this. A beautiful child to be sure, but there was something else about this one, something he couldn't put into words. More of a feeling he didn't understand.

Curious to test the child's strength, Logan placed a finger into his right palm just as he'd done with his two cousins when they were born. And while firm, he didn't find the grip any more powerful than those of his relatives. After a couple of moments, he pulled his finger away and reached for his right shoulder.

The throbbing pain where the wolf bit him had disappeared.

"Is that shoulder bothering you?" Simeon said.

Logan rubbed the wounded area. "No."

"Are you sure? You have a strange look on your face."

He bet he did. Not only had the shoulder stopped throbbing, but even when he rubbed it, he felt no pain.

"A wolf bit the boy tonight. The beast took a good piece out of his shoulder."

"How frightening," Mary said. "Would you like me to take a look at it? Perhaps put on a new dressing?"

"No, thank you," Logan said. "It's not bothering me right now."

Each of the other three shepherds took turns approaching the manger to show respect to the child. Before departing, Simeon offered a prayer of blessing over Him and thanked Mary and Joseph for the honor of visiting with them.

Logan and the others arrived back at the campsite just before daybreak. The shepherds told their sons all they had seen and heard and celebrated with them, giving glory and praises to God for the revelation spoken by the angel. The shepherds offered a slight bow of the head to Logan, declaring him a prophet because he dared to speak the name given to the Messiah before his birth.

Both embarrassed and flattered by the attention, Logan insisted he wasn't a prophet, but couldn't come up with a viable explanation the shepherds would accept. Instead, he asked them not to bow, saying it was against the customs of his own country.

"The sun will be up soon," Simeon said. "But there's still time for you to get a little sleep if you need it."

Logan couldn't sleep if he wanted to. Like the shepherds, he was too keyed up by everything that'd happened. He yawned but shook his head. "No, thanks."

"Well then, why don't we have a look at your wound? The Messiah's mother was correct. We should probably change the dressing."

Simeon helped the boy off with his jacket and shirt, then gasped.

"What?" Logan said. "What's wrong?"

"Nothing. It's just . . ." He motioned for the other shepherds to join him. They gathered around, speechless.

This was freaking him out. "Tell me what happened," Logan said.

"The wound is completely healed," Simeon said. "There is no sign of the bite or the burn."

Logan stroked his injured shoulder but felt only smooth skin and the greasiness of the salve Simeon had used to treat it. "How?"

"You touched the Christ." Simeon's voice held both certainty and awe.

The other shepherds murmured agreement.

"You mean he healed my shoulder when he grabbed my finger?"

Once more, Simeon and the other shepherds offered praises to God for the miracle they'd witnessed.

Logan's response was more restrained. He couldn't deny the astonishing nature of the things he'd experienced tonight, including the excitement of meeting the Holy Family and being healed by Jesus. But for him, even the delight of the evening had been muted by one frightful thought. If he was truly in the past, how was he going to get home? And where was Robert?

* * *

Driving to work on Christmas morning was something akin to a scene from one of those last man on earth post-apocalyptic sci-fi war films. Few walked the streets of New York City, and Marcus found the perfect parking space in the garage of the Jacob K. Javits Federal Building. He took an elevator to the 23rd floor and entered the FBI's suite of offices. There, he encountered more desolation—a darkened room full of empty desks and cubicles—before heading for his office at the far end of the floor.

After brewing a pot of coffee, Marcus pulled from a desk drawer the folder Janice had given him two days ago and separated the documents for review. He was hoping a closer examination of the forensics report and Templeton's personnel record might reveal some clue they'd overlooked. After about fifteen minutes of studying the dry lab reports his mind began to wander—all the way back to the night his wife was killed.

Carolyn had called Marcus right before leaving her parents' house in Albany, a little after four in the afternoon. Snow had started, and she wanted to be home in time to celebrate Christmas Eve at their local church. Because of the weather, Marcus had tried to talk her out of driving back that night. But she really wanted to attend church services and didn't want to miss their spending Christmas morning together. She assured him the two hour and forty-one-minute drive would bring her back in plenty of time to make the eight o'clock service.

At six o'clock, with the snow picking up, Marcus called her cell phone, only the call went directly to her voice mail. He left a message but at the time was only slightly concerned. This wasn't the first instance where she hadn't answered her phone, and she might have had the radio turned up.

By seven-forty-five, he'd begun to worry. She was now more than an hour overdue and had failed to respond to three more attempts to reach her. Even if she'd been caught in a blizzard, he should have heard back from her by then. He contacted a friend in the state police to see if he'd heard anything. In the meantime, he checked the internet for weather-related traffic updates specific to Carolyn's route home. Fifty-five minutes later, he received a call back from his state police friend advising him his wife had been involved in an accident on the Tacoma State Parkway.

"Is she all right?" Marcus said, his voice rising in volume and panic.

Silence on the other end confirmed his worst fears. His friend offered his condolences and told him Carolyn's body had been removed to the Westchester County Medical Examiner's Office in Valhalla. Marcus drove to the facility and spent the rest of the night mourning beside his wife's body, then contacted a funeral home in the morning before heading back to Staten Island.

He arrived physically and emotionally exhausted, and once inside headed straight to a cabinet in the kitchen. He removed a partially filled bottle of Jack Daniels that had been stored there for over two years. He sat at the kitchen table and polished off most of the container in twenty minutes.

Before going up to bed, he carried the last of his glass of liquor into the living room and stood in front of their eight-foot Christmas tree. He scanned its full height, unsure whether the twinkling of the lights was real or due to some alcohol-induced hallucination. He bent to pick up a package with Carolyn's name on the gift tag, only to quickly drop it onto the floor. Marcus lifted his glass and swallowed the last of the Jack, then grabbed the tree near the top and pulled it to the floor. Lights and ornaments flew everywhere, some breaking against the hardwood surface, others rolling across it.

He walked to the fireplace hearth where his wife had placed their oversized indoor Nativity scene. Always her favorite, Carolyn did her best to ensure this depiction of the birth of Christ remained a focal point of their Christmas celebration. It was the first decoration they put up each year, and the last they took down.

Marcus kicked through the crèche, shattering the wooden stable, the wings on one of the angels, and several of the animal figurines. On his way upstairs to bed, he pulled down the lighted garland wrapping the banister.

Four months after Carolyn's death, Marcus sold the house and moved to an apartment in the city. That next Christmas, he decided it was better to spend December 25th working in the office than to stay home fixating on his loss.

Marcus startled. A phone ringing on one of the desks outside his office brought him back to the present. *Who would call here on Christmas? Stupid question. I'm here.* He focused on the reports, this time concentrating on

Private Templeton's personnel record in the hope of gaining some insight into the man's character. What would a soldier with an unblemished service record, a Medal of Honor winner no less, want with a nine-year-old boy anyway?

CHAPTER II

December 26

The next morning, a confused Logan walked among the sheep trying to make sense of the previous night's events. Sure, his mother and television had taught him a few things about Jesus, but he'd also learned to be skeptical from his stepfather. Like so many of his Jewish friends, his stepdad suspected Jesus was a historical guy who did good deeds but nothing else. Certainly not the Son of God. But could such a man heal just by touching? Until now, he wasn't sure what his beliefs were about Jesus. Both his parents had made strong arguments. But after last night, he wanted to know more.

He turned to the sound of an approaching Simeon, who had a piece of clothing draped over his arm.

"You've been out here by yourself since we returned from Bethlehem. Is something troubling you?"

"A lot of things, but mostly how I'm going to get home."

"What about your friend Robert? Did he not say when he was coming back?"

"All he said was he'd be around. But now I'm

beginning to wonder."

"Perhaps this will raise your spirits. I came to tell you we will be leaving for the high pastures near Jerusalem early tomorrow morning."

Before yesterday, Logan would've been thrilled at the prospect. But since learning about being in another time, he received the news with indifference. What good would traveling to Jerusalem do now? No one there could tell him how to return to his own time. In fact, they might think he was crazy. He dropped his chin. "Oh."

"This does not please you?"

"You already told me they don't have an embassy there."

"What I said was I had never heard the word before. That doesn't mean there is not one. Either way, many wise men are in Jerusalem. Perhaps one of them might know of a way to get you back to New York."

"Not unless one of them has a time machine."

"Ah. Another word I've never heard. Something from the future?"

"Never mind." He didn't know how he was going to get home, but right now, he was thinking about Jesus. Logan had received more from his encounter with the Christ child than just a healed shoulder. "You remember yesterday when you were telling me about Micah?"

"I do."

"You said your prophets predicted the Messiah's coming. Does that mean there were other prophecies about Jesus?"

"Yes."

"Will you teach me about them?"

A smile crossed the old man's face. "Of course. But first, why don't we put your new skills to work by helping me milk a few of these sheep. Here." He handed the boy a beige tunic.

"What's this for?"

"I borrowed it from Asher for you to wear to Jerusalem tomorrow. It may be a little big, but since we have no sandals to fit you, the extra length will help to hide those shoes. The last thing we want to do is draw attention to ourselves."

Would attention to them be a problem? But Logan didn't ask.

Hours later, after they'd finished their chores and enjoyed a dinner of freshly curdled cheese and dried figs, Simeon opened another scroll of the Scriptures. Beginning in the book of Deuteronomy, he laid out the entire history of the coming Messiah as recorded by the prophets.

"You mean Moses knew about Jesus fifteen hundred years before he was born?" Logan said.

"Yes." The shepherd went on to explain other predictions in the books of Numbers, Isaiah, Jeremiah, Daniel, and Zechariah, all in addition to the Psalms.

Fascinated so much history had been devoted to a single character, Logan peppered Simeon with questions until nearly midnight. His favorite passage, which he vowed to memorize before going to bed, was Isaiah 7:14. "If the Messiah is Jesus, why does Isaiah say He will be called Immanuel?"

"It's just another name for the Messiah, the name God chose to reveal to the prophet. In Hebrew it means God with us."

God with us. Wow.

CHAPTER 12

Logan strained his neck while admiring the great wall he and Simeon passed through on their way into Jerusalem. "Wow. How long did it take to build this?"

"I don't think anyone knows exactly. It was first built by King Solomon almost a thousand years ago."

"Awesome."

Simeon chuckled. "Another strange word."

That morning, Logan had joined the shepherds as they led their herds to a pasture about three miles southwest of Jerusalem. Simeon called it the Valley of Hinnom, and their grazing site provided them with a perfect view of the elevated city. Logan had never before seen a community surrounded by a wall. He was fascinated.

Seeing it up close, he developed an even greater appreciation for how it was built. Once through the gate, the two stepped into an open courtyard next to a large housing area marked by one-level stone homes similar to those found in Bethlehem. Dozens of men and women dressed in robes and tunics walked about the city's dirt streets, talking with one another and trading at local markets. To their left, three soldiers watched everyone's movements. They looked mean or unhappy. Except for the lack of cars, Jerusalem

looked like New York or any other American city.
"Where are we headed?"

"To the home of an old rabbi who might be able to
help us."

Logan pointed to a huge, walled area with a
tall square building in the center a little more than
midway up the city's length along the eastern wall.
When he did, his garment slid down his arm exposing
his wristwatch. "What's that up there?"

"The Holy Temple."

"You there," one of the nearby soldiers shouted.

Logan pretended not to hear.

"I said, you there. Boy. Come over here."

Simeon accompanied Logan to meet the soldiers.
"How can we be of service to the king's soldiers
today?"

"What's that thing on the boy's wrist?"

Logan looked first to Simeon, who nodded, then
held out his arm so the soldiers could see. "It's called
a watch."

"What does it do?"

"It tells the time."

"Oh, really." The man's eyebrows hitched, and he
glanced at his fellow soldier. "So what time is it?"

"Ten minutes after ten."

Puzzled looks crossed the soldiers' faces.

Realizing his mistake, Logan quickly calculated
the time. "I'm sorry, I meant it's a few minutes after
the fourth hour."

Shading their eyes, the three soldiers looked
skyward. "He's right," the first soldier said. "Where
did you get this watch?"

"My mother got it for me in New York."

"New York?"

"It's the name of a city in a country a great distance from here. It's . . ."

Simeon squeezed his arm.

"If Herod's soldiers will pardon us, we must be about our business." Simeon bowed slightly and pulled Logan away, leaving behind the confused soldiers.

"I'm sorry, Simeon. I should have been more careful."

"No need to apologize. It is my fault. I should have told you to leave your watch back in camp."

"Did I tell them too much?"

The shepherd glanced back over his shoulder. "Let's just keep moving."

He led Logan to a small stone house with a flat clay-tiled roof located in the lower part of the city, not far from the gate where they entered. A man much older than Simeon greeted them at the arched doorway. He had white hair, a much longer beard, and wore a white tunic with two blue stripes running from both shoulders to his feet. "Rabbi," Simeon said, kissing his hand.

"Simeon, my dear old friend. How neglectful you've been not to come for a visit. But we can discuss that later. Who is this young man with you?"

"This is Logan. He is from a . . . another country."

"No one is a foreigner in this house. But come in, both of you." The man escorted them inside to a small wooden table with several stools. "You must be thirsty after such a journey." He poured them each a cup of water before addressing Logan. "My name is Levi. And my house is your house."

"Thank you, sir." Logan started to sit, but Simeon gently grabbed his upper arm. Once Levi sat, the shepherd released Logan so the two could join him.

"Now, how can I be of service?" Levi said.

"Rabbi." Simeon's voice filled with quiet excitement. "I think we found the Messiah." Simeon described the previous night's events, including the proclamation by the angel, their visit to the inn in Bethlehem, and Logan's miraculous healing.

With his elbows on the table, Levi folded his hands over his nose and closed his eyes as though praying or deep in thought. A minute later he looked up. "Tell no one in the city, lest news of the birth reach Herod's ears. He would immediately seek to destroy the child."

Simeon nodded. "Agreed."

Levi turned his attention to Logan "And as for you, young man, I am curious to know how the name of the most anticipated birth in Hebrew history should come to be revealed to a Gentile?"

Logan had been reluctant to try to explain to Mary or the shepherds. But there was something in the tone of Levi's voice, a calmness, a wisdom, like he would understand anything. "You may find this difficult to believe, or even to understand, but I'm not from this time period. I'm from the future. I was born in a city in a country not yet discovered. And where I come from, we've been celebrating the birth of Jesus for over five hundred years."

"I must admit, I was doubtful when I heard you tell Messiah's mother you were from the future," Simeon said. "But now . . ."

"You mean you believe me?" Logan's hopes rose.

"I don't know if I'm ready to go that far just yet," Simeon said, "but at least your story helps to explain why we've had so much trouble communicating. It's also the only explanation for your strange clothing."

"His clothes?" Levi said.

"Why don't you show Levi your watch and shoes."

Levi took a few moments to examine the items. "These certainly were not made with any of what we know. Where did you get them?"

"My mother and stepfather got them for me in New York, the city from the future where I'm from."

Simeon leaned forward, putting his palms on the table. "And thus the reason for our visit. Does Jerusalem have anything called an embassy? Apparently, it is a place where foreigners go to obtain help in returning to their own country. Logan was seeking to go there."

"I'm afraid neither the word nor the place is familiar to me. But I shall make inquiries." Levi touched the crystal of Logan's watch again. "Tell me, have you shown these to anyone else?"

"Only to the other shepherds in our camp," the boy said. "Oh, and some soldiers wanted to see the watch on our way into the city."

"Soldiers?" His eyes narrowed. "What did they say?"

"They wanted to know where I got it."

Levi and Simeon exchanged looks across the table. "Trouble?" Simeon said.

"It could be. You better be going."

"But we just got here." Logan pressed his lips tight.

"I know," Levi said. "but this is for your protection."

Simeon stood. "He's right, son. We should get out of the city as quickly as possible."

"Are your flocks grazing in the Valley of Hinnom?" the rabbi said.

"Yes."

"Excellent. I will join you there tomorrow. By then I will have learned all I can and perhaps have suggestions for how we can best help our young friend here."

This time Logan waited for Levi to rise before getting up, then thanked him when he and Simeon exited the house.

Levi threw them a final wave. "Do not tarry, my friends."

Logan and Simeon headed back toward the city's southwest entrance. When they reached the gate, twelve Roman soldiers rode up and surrounded them. Logan recognized three of them from their earlier encounter at the gate.

Simeon looked into the boy's eyes. "Say nothing."

He took a step in front of Logan. "For what purpose do shepherds draw the interest of the soldiers of Rome?"

"King Herod wishes to see the boy," the apparent leader of the soldiers said.

"Surely the king has more important things on his mind than one scrawny young boy."

"Perhaps, but my orders are to bring him to the palace."

"I'm his guardian. If it is the king's pleasure, I would like to accompany him."

"Only the boy."

The leader motioned to a cohort, who dismounted, lifted Logan onto his horse, and climbed on behind him.

As they rode away, Logan turned to look for the shepherd. Simeon hadn't moved, but stood with wrinkled brow, piercing eyes, and a hand covering his mouth. What could the king possibly want from him? With a dozen thoughts running through his mind, and all of them bad, Logan regretted coming to Jerusalem.

* * *

Two days following his arrest, Wendell sat at a flimsy table set up near the kitchen of his sparsely furnished apartment and watched porn on the internet. On the tabletop to his left sat eight empty cans of Pabst Blue Ribbon. To his right, a letter confirmed an offer of employment for a position as a custodian with Allied Cleaning Services, one of the city's leading janitorial firms. The letter also verified a starting date of January 3rd. *Looks like I skated on the arrest. Whoo, whoo.* It was time to celebrate, and he couldn't think of a better way to do it than with a twelve-pack of PBR and a screen full of smut.

For Wendell, this was a dream job, and not just because it paid more than the $11.09 per hour he currently received as a dishwasher. Allied held the contract to clean the Conservative News Channel Studios at Rockefeller Center in Midtown Manhattan, and Wendell had been assigned to a crew working the night shift. He'd always imagined working at the right-leaning news outlet and hoped to one day uncover some secret to expose them for the religious sympathizing frauds they were.

Wendell chugged down a full beer, let out a tremendous belch, and hit the play button on his computer screen to start the next movie.

CHAPTER 13

The soldiers marched Logan into the Great Hall. Jerusalem's wall paled next to the majesty of Herod's palace. Two rows of four-story-high columns surrounded him on either side of the spacious, multi-colored marble floor.

At the far end of the hall, a man with gray and black streaked hair dressed in a purple, scarlet, and gold-trimmed robe sat on a throne. A gold crown rested on his head. The seat was huge with sharp corners and made of gold. At least Logan thought it was gold. Four wide steps led to the top. Six men, all wearing varying-colored robes, surrounded the chair.

Four of the original twelve soldiers escorted Logan to the bottom of the steps beneath the throne. They saluted the man on the seat with a fisted arm thrown across their chests. "Hail Herod," the four said together.

"I am told you wear a bracelet that is able to tell the time of day," Herod said.

Logan's knees knocked. He couldn't speak.

"Is this true?"

"Y-y-yes, sir."

The king motioned to one of his advisors, who descended the staircase and removed the watch from

Logan's wrist, then carried it to Herod. The king examined the watch, repeatedly pushing the button to light up the face. "Who are these people dressed in red and black?"

"The Incredibles."

"Incredibles. Are they your gods?"

"They're superheroes."

"Your words mean nothing." The king played with the watch like it was a toy. "So how does this thing tell you where the sun is in the sky?"

Even though he knew Herod wouldn't understand what English numbers were or how to read them, Logan feared not giving an answer. "The black numbers indicate the time."

"These figures, they are not Hebrew, Latin, or even Greek. Are they the language of the nation you come from?"

"Yes."

"And where is this nation?"

"It's all the way on the other side of the world, across the ocean. It's called the United States of America."

"You speak strangely, boy. What is your name?"

"Logan."

"Even your name is strange."

Another of the advisors, this one wearing a black robe trimmed in silver and a fancy headpiece, whispered in Herod's ear. Logan assumed he was some sort of priest.

"Last night, a new star appeared over Bethlehem," the priest said. "We believe the star proclaims the arrival of the Messiah, as foretold by our prophets in the Scriptures.

"What does this have to do with me?" Logan said.

The priest stepped slowly down the stairs and stood glaring over him. "I was just wondering if it is a coincidence, you show up in Israel at this point in time."

Logan lifted his head, his voice confident. "I didn't just show up. I've been here for six days."

"So you say. But let us consider what we know. Here's a boy who comes from a place no one has ever heard of, wearing a bracelet no one has ever seen, at the exact time as the arrival of the prophetic star."

Oh, man. This guy thinks I'm the Messiah. "Surely you don't think I'm — "

"My lord." The priest turned to Herod. "This boy knows more than he is telling. He should be interrogated under anguish."

Herod put a finger to his lips. "This requires careful thought. The people have been waiting centuries for the Anointed One. But we must be sure."

"All the more reason to begin interrogating the boy as soon as possible."

"There's plenty of time for that. For now, take him to the dungeons of the Citadel. Guard him carefully. Oh, and see that he's not given any food or water. Perhaps that will serve to pry the truth from his lips."

The four soldiers led Logan from the palace, across a large open courtyard, and down a long dirt street ending at the entrance to an enormous block building. It reminded Logan of a medieval fort or castle. He was turned over to a jailer who placed him in a dark, smelly cell made — with the exception of its iron door — completely of stone. The odor reminded him of his grandparents mildewed basement and the boy's locker room at school following gym class.

After the jailor shut the door, Logan sat on some

straw provided for his bed and cried. This morning, his biggest fear had been how he was going to get home. Now he was worried about where he was going to get his next meal. Add to this he'd lost his prized *Incredibles 2* watch, and it had been a bad day all-around. On the other hand, scared as he'd been, the idea of being mistaken for Jesus gave him a strange but good feeling.

He laid back on the straw to take a nap. For the second time in five days, hunger pangs descended upon him.

* * *

December 28

Without his watch, Logan couldn't tell how long he'd gone without food or water. And with only a small window in the cell, it was nearly impossible for him to distinguish between night and day. Not only was his throat dry and his stomach cramped, but also weakness and lightheadedness had overtaken him. For the first time since arriving back in time, he experienced a real fear he wouldn't make it back home. How long had he been here? Two days he figured. The soldiers had been dousing the torches at night, and he'd been keeping track of the guard changes, which had taken place three times a day before he'd see a familiar face again.

He tried hard to distract himself and keep his mind off his hunger. But with his tongue sticking to the roof of his mouth and his stomach rumbling like a storm cloud, he wasn't having much luck. He'd even tried eating a piece of straw but found it too dry and tasteless to swallow. Out in the hallway, a guard extinguished all but a single torch. Facing another night without food, Logan thought about something he hadn't done since he was a toddler but had seen the shepherd do the first day they met. He didn't know if he could do it right but felt like he wanted to try. Logan kneeled on his bed of straw and folded his hands on his chest, then offered the very first prayer ever spoken on his own.

"Dear God. I'm hungry, thirsty, and really, really scared. But I guess you already know that because you're God. If You could please find a way to send me some food and water, I'd really appreciate it. Amen."

Logan turned to the sound of laughter coming from the hallway. The guard, whose mouth was full of blackened and crooked teeth, pressed his face against the cell door window. "Well, isn't that sweet? What are you wasting your time praying for? Besides, I've got some good news for you. Come tomorrow, you won't have to worry about being hungry anymore."

"Did the king change his mind about giving me food?" Logan said.

"Not exactly. Earlier today, I saw Jabal the Executioner having his sword sharpened at the blacksmith's. He said he was ordered to have it ready to behead a prisoner in the morning. And I don't know of anyone else being held here who's been condemned lately." The guard backed away from the window laughing.

Logan's lips quivered. *They're going to kill me?*

Last night, with a cramping stomach keeping him awake, a plan to save himself leaped into his mind. What if he were to tell Herod about the real Messiah, including His whereabouts at the inn in Bethlehem?

Surely the king would be grateful, perhaps even provide him with a banquet to feast upon. But before he'd had time to fully consider the matter, he'd fallen asleep.

But things were different now, he was to be executed in the morning.

Logan rose from his straw bed and started for the door to summon the guard. Then he remembered the words of Levi who warned that Herod would most certainly kill the Child if he found Him. *How could I do such a horrible thing?* He walked back and forth between the door and his bed three times before falling to his knees again to offer his second prayer in the last five minutes.

"Oh, Lord, I know if I tell where to find the Messiah, I'll probably get some food. But I also believe what Levi said that telling would put Him in danger. Won't You please give me the strength to do the right thing? And while You're at it, I could still use some food down here. Amen."

Before his interaction with the guard, weakness from a lack of nourishment had actually made Logan tire. But sleep now? Not likely. Not with the prospect of beheading waiting for him in the morning. *Robert, where are you?*

CHAPTER 14

In the morning, Wendell stood in front of the mirror in his bathroom popping zits. Pizza face. That's what the kids in high school used to call him, and with good reason. "Whoa," he said, pressing another whitehead between his fingertips and watching it splatter onto the glass. "I may have to offer free delivery on this one."

But making fun of Wendell's face wasn't the only thing his classmates used to tease him about. They thought he was weird, partly because of the way he dressed but more for the way he acted. He'd wear the same clothes two, sometimes three days in a row and think nothing of it. One day, one of the guys asked him about it, so he leaned his head over as far as he could to sniff his underarms. "Smells okay to me," he said.

He also had a habit of wearing mismatched socks but couldn't understand why that would bother anyone. No one looked at his feet anyway. Girls thought he was creepy because he was always coming up behind them and smelling their hair. Boys thought he was strange because he didn't like sports or show any interest in talking about girls. Almost everyone considered him a loner, probably because he never made any effort to make friends or join the others in after school social activities.

Now, with his face culling completed, Wendell took a moment to examine the lump over his left eye. While the swelling had gone down considerably over the past four days, it remained sensitive to the touch. He picked up a toothbrush with flattened bristles to brush his teeth, then ran a comb through his greasy brown hair before exiting the bathroom.

He approached a calendar hanging on a wall near the kitchen. December 29th. Two days until New Year's Eve, one of his favorite holidays. Wendell looked forward to celebrating the New Year, but not for the same reason most people did. For him, it was all about the fireworks displays, particularly the explosions and colorful showers painting the night sky. He loved explosions, and although the city deemed it illegal to possess them, he had a half brick of 640 Black Cat firecrackers saved for the occasion.

Actually, New Year's was only Wendell's second favorite holiday, his first being July fourth, a time when the fireworks displays were larger, grander, and most importantly, louder. Years ago, before he left home as a teenager, his parents had taken him to a place in South Carolina called South of the Border. Best known for its reputation as a tourist trap, it was also home to one of the largest and most widely assorted fireworks collections on the east coast. There, the would-be fireworks bug could find everything needed to start out any holiday with a bang—firecrackers, cherry bombs, M-80s, bottle rockets. Wendell had spent his entire vacation allowance there, then borrowed money from his parents to purchase another twenty dollars' worth.

Next to the calendar stood a cheap, veneer-covered, pressed-wood bookcase filled with writings from many of the great Atheist philosophers like Friedrich Engels, John Dewey, and Jeremy Bentham. The library included books from some contemporary atheists as well: *The God Delusion* by Richard Dawkins, *All That's Wrong with the Bible* by Jonah David Conner, and *Why There is No God* by Armin Navabi. In addition to these works, Wendell had recently added biographical narratives about domestic terrorists Timothy McVeigh and Ted Kaczynski. Most days, he would take a book with him to read during his break in his current job as a dishwasher at a small diner in Chelsea.

Wendell moved to the bookcase and chose the book, *American Terrorist, Timothy McVeigh and the Oklahoma City Bombing*, from the shelf and headed out the door.

* * *

Logan startled when he heard the jingle of a key unlocking his cell door. The time had come for his execution. He sat up in his straw bed. A man in a maroon tunic carrying a torch entered the cell and put a finger to his lips. Logan recognized him as one of the advisors from Herod's court.

"Come with me," he whispered.

"Where?" Logan said.

"The king intends to have you executed in the morning. This, I cannot allow."

"You would risk your own neck to defy Herod. Why?"

"I am a Jew, as are others within Herold's circle. If you are the Messiah, we cannot allow the king to destroy you just to protect his own rule." He gestured toward the open door. "Come, we must move quickly."

"What about the guard?"

"He likes wine, and I've supplied him plenty. He's passed out."

Logan followed the advisor out of the cell and down the corridor. Against the far wall with two empty wineskins at his feet, the guard snored loudly.

The man led Logan through the dark tunnels, up a narrow staircase, and out the entrance to the castle, where they passed two more sleeping guards. They moved down the street and around a corner to a small open area. A donkey stood tethered to an iron gate. "You'll find food and water on the animal," the man said.

Logan spread his hands, palms up, and shrugged. "I don't know how to thank you."

"You just did. Do you think you can find your way back to where the shepherds are camped?

Logan scanned the area. He recognized enough landmarks to feel confident. "I think so, yes."

"See to it you escape so you can grow into the man who will one day set Israel free." The advisor reached into his tunic and handed Logan his watch. "I liberated this from the king when he fell asleep."

Logan thanked him, strapped on the watch, and checked the time. Three-fifty-five a.m., Israeli time.

The advisor bowed at Logan's feet. "Lord, please remember this kindness."

Not knowing how to respond, Logan paused for a moment before nodding. "I will."

Logan rode his donkey back through the southwest gate and on to the pasture where they'd left the herds. When he entered the camp, all of the shepherds and their sons ran to greet him. Simeon helped him off the animal before giving him a hug. "Are you all right, son?" He looked him up and down. "How did you get back here?"

Logan shared the details of his ordeal and release with the help of the advisor.

Simeon exchanged a look of concern with the other shepherds. "We don't have much time. As soon as Herod learns of his escape, he'll send his soldiers here after him."

"What are you going to do?" Eliab said.

"The way I see it, we have two choices, flee or hide."

"But which one?" Logan said.

Simeon retrieved a knife, separated a large male sheep from the rest of the herd, and slit its throat.

CHAPTER 15

Even in the cooler temperatures, Logan sweated beneath the blanket of his camouflage to the sound of the thunderous arrival of Herod's soldiers. He strained to hear the leader above the sound of bleating sheep, all while trying to remain deathly still.

"Seize them all." The commanding voice was deep and confident.

"Who do you seek?" Simeon said.

"The boy who came to Jerusalem with you. Where is he?"

"He's not here. And unless I'm mistaken, were you not one of the soldiers who took him to the palace?"

"Search the camp."

Blinded by his covering and the instructions given him by Simeon, Logan had to rely on his hearing to figure out what was going on. Sounds of rummaging, the tearing of canvas and leather, and the smashing of pottery filled his ears.

"Claudius. Take a dozen men and walk through these flocks, just in case he's hiding there."

Logan's heart raced, and his hands turned clammy. Simeon had hidden him among one of the largest groups of sheep, hoping their sheer numbers would be enough to camouflage him. But now, with the soldiers entering the herd, some of the animals nearest him began to move about. Limited to movement on his hands and knees, he tried to stay close to the other sheep, but was having difficulty. Aggravating the situation, the voices of the soldiers conversing with one another drew closer and closer.

Ten agonizing minutes later, the boy flinched at the sound of a soldier's voice only a few yards behind him. Certain he would be discovered, he wondered if he should try crawling away.

"There's nothing here but these stinking sheep," the soldier said, his voice nearly on top of him. Come on, let's get back to camp."

Relieved, Logan remained motionless. That was until the commander announced his intentions.

"He couldn't have gotten far, not a boy his age. Claudius, take half the men and head east, to Jericho. The rest of us will head west, to Kirjath Jearim.

"And let me tell you shepherds something. You had better hope we don't find out the boy came back here. Because if we do, I'll come back and cut all three of your son's throats. All right, let's move out."

Logan waited until the sound of the soldiers' horses faded in the distance before rising from the pasture and throwing off his disguise. He stood, half naked, looking down at the wooly skin of an adult sheep, complete with the head and tail still attached.

The three shepherds and their sons hurried toward him. Simeon handed Logan his original clothes. "Quickly now, put these on. You need to be gone before the soldiers return."

"Gone where?" Logan said.

"I want you to take your camel and head south

to Bethany, a small town that Herod's soldiers might easily overlook. When you get there, ask for a man named Demas. He is my brother. He will help you. He also knows Levi and will be able to get word to him."

"But aren't you coming with me?"

Simeon glanced in the direction of the departed soldiers. "Those soldiers know I was with you in Jerusalem. And when they don't find you in Jericho or Kirjath Jearim, their next move will be to return. If I'm not here, they will know I was lying and cause them to search all the harder to find you."

Logan dressed hastily and offered a hurried good-bye and hug to each of the other shepherds and their sons.

Not so with Simeon. He wrapped his arms around the man's waist and seemed unable to let go. "I'm going to miss you," he said, the warmth of a tear staining his cheek.

"I will miss you as well, my son."

"I learned so much."

Simeon gently broke Logan's grip, pushing away so he could look him in the face. His own eyes welled. "If so, then use that learning to help you become the best person you can be."

"I will. I promise."

Simeon helped Logan onto his camel, then patted him on the leg. "May God go with you."

"Good-bye."

Twenty minutes later, Logan rode his camel due southeast of Jerusalem. Soon the profile of a small town appeared in the distance. Cresting a rise, he looked down to where a man in a green jacket sat on a camel at the bottom of the hill just outside the city.

The boy wasn't close enough to make out the man's features, and for a moment he thought of fleeing in another direction. But there was something strangely familiar about the man, and he proceeded down the hill.

When he got within thirty yards, Logan's mouth dropped open in recognition of his guide, Robert. "Where in the world have you been? Do you have any idea what I've been through?"

Robert paused and smiled. "It's time for you to go home."

"Great. Are we going back the same way we got here?"

"Well, I'm not going to ask you to close your eyes and tap your heels together three times, if that's what you're thinking."

Logan leaned forward in the saddle. "Tell me something, did you really bring me back here just to prove to me Christmas is about more than getting presents?"

"Partly. Logan, you have been approved by God."

"Approved for what?"

"Just as Paul was a chosen vessel to spread the message of the Gospel, so are you a chosen vessel to spread the message of Christmas."

First, he was being mistaken for Jesus. Now he was being asked by God to carry a message, and it frightened him. "Who am I that God would chose me? My family doesn't even go to church or read the Bible."

"The Lord is concerned about the diluting of the Christmas message over the years. He believes a reminder might be better received if delivered by the mouth of a child."

"What does He want me to do?"

"Very simple. Just go back and tell people what you saw."

"And what makes you think people are going to believe *me*?"

Robert laughed. "Many will not. But then again, many will. Are you ready?"

"I guess so." After his close call with Herod, Logan was definitely ready to go home. He wasn't as sure about being the one chosen to deliver a message from God.

* * *

Marcus thanked Mrs. Thomas for the morning coffee. He sat in the living room with Janice and Todd, who'd spent another night monitoring the surveillance equipment. The lines in their faces showed their exhaustion.

"It's been nine days." Karen set the tray of coffee on the end table beside the sofa. "Don't you think we should have heard something by now if our son had been kidnapped?"

Marcus was impressed. If the Thomases were involved in their son's disappearance, they were certainly putting on a good front. "Not necessarily." He passed coffee to the agents sitting in chairs on either side of the couch. "Some of these people have been known to delay contacting the victim's family as part of a strategy to heighten their anxiety. Then, when contact is finally initiated, the families are so elated they forget all about negotiation and accede to whatever ransom demands are made."

Karen's parents, and her younger sister took their

coffee at a kitchen table adjacent to the living room. The family had flown in from Kentucky a week ago. As for the other half dozen friends who'd shown up during the initial days of the investigation, Marcus had politely asked them to go home. He feared their presence might prove a distraction to the surveillance activities.

"Surely, there must be something else we can do." Brad sighed deeply, tilting his head back. "This waiting is unbearable."

Everyone's attention was drawn to the sound of a thump coming from Logan's bedroom, followed by the door opening and the boy walking out.

"Logan!" Mrs. Thomas screamed. Her exclamation was quickly echoed by her parents and sister, who joined Mr. Thomas in rushing to hug the missing child. Together, the family peppered him with questions of "What happened to you? Where have you been? Are you all right? How did you get back?" None of which the boy was given time to answer.

Marcus couldn't believe it. How did the boy get into his room without being seen? He sent Todd and Janice to check the bedroom while he joined the reunion. Mrs. Thomas introduced Logan to the agent and explained how he was the person heading up the investigation into his disappearance. He extended his hand. "Glad to see you're safe, young man. You've had an awful lot of folks out looking for you." While shaking Logan's hand, he noticed the tears in the shoulder of his jacket. "What's this blood from?"

"Blood!" Mrs. Thomas said. She and her husband crowded in around Logan.

"That's where the wolf bit me," Logan said.

Mrs. Thomas's eyes widened. "A wolf bit you?"

"Yeah, but it's all healed now."

Mr. Thomas picked through the tears to his jacket and shirt at the skin underneath. "There's nothing here."

"Well, the important thing is you're okay," Mrs. Thomas said.

Following this short pause, the madness of machine gun questioning to the boy by his family resumed until Mr. Thomas finally raised both a hand and his voice. "Hold on, just a minute everyone. Logan, where have you been?"

The boy turned to his mom. "Mom, remember that homeless guy we met outside the Chick-Fil-A the other day?"

"The man in the army jacket, the one you gave your food to?" Mrs. Thomas said. "Yes."

"Well, he turned out to be an angel. And he took me back in time to see the birth of Jesus."

A hush enveloped the room, and six pairs of widened eyes stared at Logan.

Mrs. Thomas broke the silence. "An angel?"

"Yeah," Logan said. "An angel named Robert."

"And you say this angel took you back in time to see Jesus?"

"That's right, Mom. Just like we learned in Sunday school. There was a stable. And there were animals lying all around. And Mary and Joseph were there. And the baby Jesus was lying on a bed of straw in a manger. Just like the Nativity Scenes people put up at Christmas."

Karen's father motioned to his daughter. "Check the boy for a head injury."

Mrs. Thomas kneeled to look directly into Logan's eyes, then manipulated her fingers along his skull and beneath his hair to examine it. She shook her head. "I don't see anything."

"Perhaps it's just a child's fantasy," Karen's mother said.

"It's no fantasy, Grandma. I really did get to meet Jesus."

Mr. Thomas's face tightened. "I don't know what this is all about, Logan, but there are no such things as angels."

"Oh, yes there are, Dad. And not just Robert. I saw thousands of them."

Curious as he was to hear what the boy had to say, Marcus had an investigation to conduct and a mystery to uncover. "If I could interrupt for just a moment." He turned to the boy's parents. "Mr. and Mrs. Thomas. Rather than ask Logan to tell his story twice, I'd like to have the three of you accompany us to headquarters so we can take a formal statement."

"Now?" Karen said. "But he just got home."

Marcus nodded. "Our investigation begins and ends with your son. It's critical we obtain as much information about what happened to him while it's still fresh in his mind."

"I don't know. What do you think, Brad?"

"I think we should ask him." Mr. Thomas looked down at Logan. "How about it? Do you feel up to sit for an interview with these guys?"

"Sure, Dad. I feel fine."

"Good," Agent Garraway said. "We'll treat you to lunch at the office cafeteria, or . . ." The senior agent winked at Mrs. Thomas. "How about we have lunch brought in from Chick-Fil-A?"

Logan's eyes lit up. "The Chick? Definitely."

"You got it."

When Todd and Janice exited Logan's bedroom, Marcus led them over to the foyer for privacy. From the stoic looks on their faces, he could tell they hadn't found anything. Janice gave a slight shake of the head. "Nothing out of the ordinary," she said. "Looks clean."

"And you're both sure the boy couldn't have gotten back into his bedroom sometime last night?"

"Not a chance," Todd said. "Nobody's come through that front door, and Janice and I checked the boy's room multiple times during the night when making our rounds."

"Okay. Just the same, get the technicians down here to go over everything again." Marcus's journey into the twilight zone continued. Though genuinely relieved at the boy's safe return, the investigation into what happened to him was likely to remain arduous. Especially if he stuck to his current story. In the meantime, Logan's reappearance seemed to pose more questions than his disappearance, starting with . . . How on earth did he get back into that bedroom?

Agent Fowlkes pulled out her cell phone to make the call.

"And Janice," Marcus leaned in to whisper in her ear, "tell them to bring whatever equipment is necessary to do a complete physical examination of the apartment. I want them to look for any secret passages, doorways, pull-downs, or trap doors that may be hidden in the walls, ceiling, or floor. And not just in the boy's room but the entire apartment. Any place where a person might conceal themselves. And tell them I don't care how big a mess they make doing it."

CHAPTER 16

Marcus exited the door to the FBI's main investigative offices to where the Thomases had been waiting on a bench for about fifteen minutes. This followed a nearly two-hour interview of Logan in their presence conducted by Agents Fowlkes and Curtis, after which the parents were asked to wait out in the hallway. Marcus joined them on the bench. He sat in silence, hands folded on his lap.

"Where's Logan?" Mrs. Thomas said, squirming in her seat.

Marcus glanced toward the door. "He'll be right out. We had to take the jacket and shirt your son was wearing to send to the lab. The copper coin, too. Todd and Janice are getting him some other clothes to wear."

A pinched expression appeared on Mr. Thomas's face. "Why? "You're not buying that yarn he told about being attacked by a wolf are you? You saw his shoulder. There wasn't a mark on it."

"No, but his jacket and shirt were ripped and had blood on them. And whether we believe it or not, we have an obligation to use every means at our disposal to either confirm or refute his story. An analysis of those items should tell us something."

"What story?" Mr. Thomas said. "That was more like a fairytale."

"Do you mind if I ask you about your family's religious background?"

"We don't have one," Mr. Thomas said. "My wife was raised a Baptist, but she's not practicing."

"What about your son?"

"Certainly not."

Mrs. Thomas touched her husband's hand. "When Logan was a preschooler," she said, "I used to read to him from a children's Bible and let him watch Veggie Tales videos. Later, he attended Sunday school up until a couple of years ago when he seemed to lose interest."

"So, he'd be familiar with the Christmas story?" Marcus said.

"Absolutely. But why he'd use it as an excuse to explain where he's been the past nine days, I don't know. And all that stuff about Simeon and the shepherds, Levi, and Herod putting him in a dungeon, none of that's a part of the Christmas story."

"Granted. But I've got to be honest with you, Mrs. Thomas. I've interviewed a lot of missing children in my career. And I can tell you from experience that the ones who lie always have a problem relaying their story."

"What do you mean?"

"To begin with, they fidget, and they have trouble looking you in the eye. They either stutter, stammer, or forget something they told you previously during the interview. I didn't see any of that with Logan. He maintained strict eye contact throughout, and recounted his story with unhesitating clarity and confidence, as though he'd absolutely lived through it."

Mr. Thomas stood and glared down at Marcus. "You're not saying you believe him?"

"No, but I do think *he* believes it."

"Oh, great, so he's crazy."

"Brad." Mrs. Thomas raised her voice.

"I'm not saying that either," Marcus said. "But there could be something pathological or delusional in the boy's thinking. In which case, you might want to consider taking him to a child psychologist."

Mrs. Thomas put her head in her hands. "Oh, no."

"On the other hand, it could be just what your mother suggested back at the apartment. Logan is just living out a fantasy. One that over time, he'll probably lose interest in."

Mr. Thomas ran a hand through his hair. "What do we do in the meantime?"

"Be patient. And remember, as of now, we don't know what may have happened to him over those nine days. Where he was. Who he may have been with. He doesn't appear to have suffered any physical injury, but until he's willing to be more forthcoming about his ordeal, we won't know for sure."

"All right. We'll be patient." Mr. Thomas pointed to the door leading back to the interview rooms. "But it's going to take a lot more than some behavioral or psychological analysis of that boy to explain how he disappeared from his bedroom. Or, how he magically reappeared."

"I know. That's why we're continuing with our investigation in spite of your son's story."

Mr. Thomas sat next to his wife. "So, Agent Garraway, can I ask why you wanted Karen and I to wait out here while you completed Logan's interview?"

"We had to ask your son questions that, quite frankly, we thought he might be hesitant to answer if you were present."

"What kind of questions?"

"Questions related to your own involvement in the case."

Mr. and Mrs. Thomas stared wide-eyed at each other. "Oh," Mr. Thomas said. "We didn't know we were suspects."

"We didn't know either. That's why we had to ask *him* the questions." Marcus preferred to have kept them as unwitting suspects. But then, there would have been no way for the agents to keep Logan from tipping over the bean can once he got home.

The door across the hall opened, and Logan walked out carrying a Chick-fil-A soda cup and wearing a slightly oversized FBI T-shirt and jacket. Agents Fowlkes and Curtis followed close behind. "Hey, look at this cool shirt and jacket they gave me. Just like real FBI agents wear."

Mr. Thomas fingered the jacket sleeve. "That's great, Logan."

Marcus walked them to the elevator at the end of the hall. "I'll call you in a couple of days, sooner if there's a break in the case. For now, Todd and Janice will take you home and remove the surveillance equipment from your apartment."

Mrs. Thomas thanked him before entering the elevator with her family and the two agents.

No sooner had the elevator door closed than Marcus's angst began at his having to wait until tomorrow morning to discuss the interview with his team. And yet, there was one aspect of the boy's story that puzzled him more than anything else, including its fantastic nature. Logan's description of his guide back in time, Robert, sounded an awful lot like the stranger he'd met in the cemetery just a few days ago.

* * *

With his parents, grandparents, and aunt all seated around him in the living room, Logan kneeled beneath the tree to open his mountain of gifts. Despite having his Christmas delayed for four days, rather than tear into them as he was accustomed, he slowly opened each present.

Earlier in the evening, the family had gathered around the TV to watch the press coverage of Logan's return. Agent Garraway and an NYPD Deputy Chief of Police spoke from a podium set up inside the lobby of the FBI building. Video showing the outside of the Thomases building ran on a continuous loop during the broadcast. All the police would say was that Logan had returned safely, and the circumstances of his disappearance were still under investigation.

"Logan, are you feeling okay?" Mom said.

"Sure," Logan said. "Why?"

"I guess we're just used to seeing you attack your gifts like a contestant in a pie-eating contest, but tonight you don't seem to be in any big hurry."

Logan opened a box containing the Mr. Incredible action figure before laying it on the floor. "Mom, why do we exchange gifts at Christmas?"

His mother paused a moment before speaking. "Many people believe the tradition of gift-giving is rooted in pagan ritual. But Christians believe Christmas started with a gift, the gift of God's only Son, Jesus. And our presents to each other are a commemoration of that first gift."

Dad peeked over the top edge of his newspaper while seated on the couch. "Oh, please, Karen. Don't tell him that. If you're going to start preaching, I'm going back to the bedroom."

"Why don't you just read your paper?" Mom said.

"Well, if Christmas is about Jesus," Logan said, flicking one of the many Santa Claus ornaments on the tree, "then who started all this Santa Claus stuff?"

"It's called commercialization," she said, "and it began almost a hundred years ago. Basically, it says a jolly old fat man in a red suit and white beard makes a better spokesman for advertisers than a humble prophet in a robe."

"But Santa isn't real."

"No, but he is based on someone who was. You've heard of Saint Nicholas?"

"Sure, Saint Nick."

"Well, unlike Santa Claus, Saint Nicholas was a real person, a Christian bishop who lived in the late third to early fourth century. He was known for secretly giving gifts to the needy. Over time, the real Saint Nicholas morphed into the legendary character we know today as Santa Claus."

"A lot of people think Jesus isn't real either," Dad said.

Logan's grandfather snorted. "You're the only one in this room, Brad."

"Oh, no, Dad," Logan said. "Jesus is real. I saw him with my own eyes."

"That's my grandson." Granddad's scowl turned into a broad smile.

"Sure. If you say so." Dad stood, folded his newspaper, and headed for his and Mom's bedroom.

No sooner had Dad closed the door than Logan stopped opening gifts and walked around the tree, examining one ornament and then another. "We sure do have a lot of Santa Claus ornaments."

Mom joined him. "I never paid that much attention."

"Mom, how come we've never put up a Nativity scene? All my Christian friends put one up in their homes at Christmas."

Mom looked at Grandma and Granddad then back to Logan. "I suppose it's because I'm always so busy with shopping, cooking, and decorating, I never had the time to go looking for the right one. A Nativity scene is like a Bible — it's a very personal item."

"Ah, come on Karen," Granddad said, "don't sugar coat it for the boy. Tell him the truth. It's because that husband of yours doesn't want one."

Logan's grandmother touched him on the arm. "That's their business, Martin."

"Given that Christmas is really about Jesus," Logan said, "don't you think we should?"

His mother smiled and nodded. "You're absolutely right."

He hugged her and moved around the room to give hugs to his grandparents and aunt. "Thank you all for the neat presents." He headed for his bedroom.

"Where are you going?" Mom pointed to the pile of gifts, half were unopened.

"To bed. I'm tired."

"Don't you want to finish opening your presents?"

"They'll still be there tomorrow."

Exhausted from the past nine days, Logan got ready for sleep. Though happy to be home and in his own bed, he already missed his new friends, especially Simeon. But Logan's presence in their camp no longer presented a danger to them. Herod's soldiers may have returned, but without Logan, they had no evidence to accuse the shepherds of helping him escape. And that thought comforted him greatly.

So why did he feel like crying?

CHAPTER 17

The next morning, Marcus and his team met again in the conference room on the twenty-third floor at headquarters. Janice sat in her customary seat next to Todd wearing a grin like an IRS auditor who'd just found unreported income.

"All right people," Marcus said, "we've got our boy back. Now we have to find out what happened to him. Let's start with the reprocessing of Logan's bedroom. Janice, you look like the cat who swallowed the proverbial canary."

Janice opened her binder and pulled out a report. "The evidence techs lifted the fingerprints of four individuals." Agent Fowlkes looked up from the report and nodded toward the other side of the table. "Mine and Todd's, which we expected, Logan's, of course, and . . ."

"And what?" Marcus said. "Whose are they?"

"Robert Ford Templeton's."

Jaws dropped around the table, which seemed to humor Janice, who chuckled.

"No way," Phil said. "You're telling us that not only do we have a suspect who's been dead for over seventy years, but he came back for a return engagement?"

"That's what Latent is telling us."

Imitating those cheesy TV commercials advertising cookware, sealant, and food choppers, Agent Fowlkes continued. "But wait, there's more." She pulled from the binder an old black and white photograph of a man wearing an army uniform and handed it to Marcus. "We were able to obtain this from the granddaughter of Private Templeton's sister."

Marcus took the picture, and his hands shook. The skin on his neck and back tingled. He stared at the picture for nearly thirty seconds, examining every detail of the man's face before passing it on to Todd.

"It's —" Janice said.

"Templeton," Marcus said, "yeah, I know."

She leaned across the table toward him. "You all right, boss? You look like you've seen a ghost."

Not a ghost, an angel. Marcus's suspicions had been confirmed. The man in the photograph looked exactly like the man who'd visited him in the cemetery, a detail he thought best to keep to himself for now. "I'm fine. He looks like someone I thought I may have met before, but I can't place who or where."

Todd tapped the photo against the fingertips of his other hand. "You want to try showing it to the kid?"

"What for?" Phil said. "So he can confirm the ridiculous notion that we're looking for a corpse?"

"Not just a corpse," Todd said. "But a corpse whose fingerprints keep showing up in the same place."

Marcus nodded. "Go ahead and put his picture in a line-up and see if Logan can pick him out. Let's see if his Robert and our Robert are one in the same." He turned back to Janice, who had pulled out another report.

"The good news," she said. "The lab was able to extract mitochondrial DNA from the hair samples recovered. The bad. I did some checking and found out our Robert Templeton isn't buried at Arlington Cemetery like I thought. He, and nine thousand other U.S. soldiers are interred at the Normandy American Cemetery at Colleville-sur-Mer, France."

Marcus blew air threw his lips like a horse snorting. "Okay, well before any of you start lobbying me for a trip overseas, let's see what happens with the line-up. How about the structural examination of the apartment?"

"Nothing. The floor, the walls, the ceiling—all solid, commercial-grade construction. No evidence of renovation, alteration, or tampering."

"If the integrity of the room itself hasn't been compromised, that leaves the windows as the only means of access into the room besides the door, correct?"

"Windows protected by an eighty-foot drop to the street," Todd said.

"Yeah, right." Marcus nodded slightly. "What about Logan's statement? I know the boy suffers from an overactive imagination, but surely there must be something there we can use."

Todd pulled out a copy of Logan's statement. "Did anyone else notice how close his description of Robert is to what we've learned so far about Private Templeton?"

"A clean-cut homeless guy in an army jacket and pants?" Phil said. "There's probably a few thousand guys who fit that description in New York City alone."

"What about the tears to his shirt and jacket, and the blood on them?"

"Who knows what happened? They could've gotten ripped on a barbed wire fence or something. But you saw his shoulder just like we did. Who ever heard of a wolf bite healing in six days, except maybe in one of those old werewolf movies?"

Some of the team members snickered.

"Yeah, and cuts from a barbed wire fence wouldn't have healed that quickly either," Todd said.

"I don't think we can take anything the boy said at face value," Phil said. "Not with that wild story about going back in time to see Jesus."

Janice turned to face Marcus. "What do we do now?"

"What we always do," Marcus said. "We follow the evidence, and right now the evidence still points to our late friend, Private Templeton, being in the boy's room when he disappeared *and* when he returned. In the meantime, let's hope if Logan is living out a fantasy, he tires of it quickly and gives us something more to go on."

Though he'd tried to hide it, inside, Marcus was still shaken by the face in the photograph and its resemblance to the man who'd interrupted his suicide intentions. Who was he? And if he and Templeton were the same man, what was his joint interest in a senior FBI agent and a nine-year-old boy? One thing he was fairly certain of . . . angels didn't leave fingerprints. At least he didn't think they did. Come to think of it, he never thought corpses did either. Until now.

CHAPTER 18

Logan's two-hour Minecraft marathon the next morning ended when his mother asked if he'd take a break to talk with his parents. He entered a near-empty living room — her parents and sister having flown back to Kentucky yesterday — and sat on the couch next to his stepdad.

"What's up?" Logan said.

"Your dad and I want to talk to you about some of the things you told the FBI."

"Sure."

"How did you know about all those things that took place when Jesus was born?" Mom said. "Did you remember them from our study of the Bible when you were younger, from Sunday school, or maybe see them in a movie?"

"No. I saw them myself."

"You mean you saw them in a dream," Dad said. "Is that it?"

"No. I really saw them with my own eyes. I saw baby Jesus, and the angels, and I saw Mary and Joseph."

Dad frowned. "But in a dream."

Logan shook his head. "Dad, it wasn't a dream. No more than my seeing Simeon, Levi, or Herod was a dream."

Mom took one of Logan's hands. "Do you understand the things you say you saw took place thousands of years ago?"

"If they took place at all," Dad added.

Logan's mother glared at him. "Enough with the skeptic editorial. We just want to find out what happened." She focused again on Logan.

"Yes, Mom. I know they happened a long time ago."

"And do you realize it's not possible for anyone to travel back in time?"

"I used to think that," Logan said. "When I first got there, for the first few days, I couldn't understand why Simeon and I had so much trouble understanding each other. Then, after seeing Mary, Joseph, and the baby Jesus, I realized it had to be because I'd gone back in time."

"It was a dream," Dad said. "People can't go back in time."

"What about the guy in that movie we watched, *The Time Machine*? He went back in time."

"That was a movie. Make believe. It wasn't real."

Mom touched Logan's knee. "Where did you learn all those things about what Moses and the old prophets said about Jesus? I don't remember us covering any Old Testament prophecy during our studies."

"Simeon taught me. Here, let me show you. Isaiah 7:14 says, 'Therefore the Lord Himself will give you a sign: Behold, the virgin shall conceive and bear a Son, and shall call His name Immanuel.'"

Almost as if she was proud of him, a slight smile appeared on Mom's face.

"Immanuel?" Dad said.

"It means, God-With-Us, Dad."

"Pfft," he said. "God with us. Oh, brother."

Mom's lips pinched together. "Brad, please."

Dad leveled his gaze at Logan. "Enough of this foolishness. I want you to tell me the truth. Who filled your head with all this religious stuff? Did someone threaten you if you didn't agree to tell us this cockamamie story?"

Logan sighed. "I told you, Simeon taught me part of it. And the rest I saw with my own two eyes."

Red-faced, Dad stood and stormed into the kitchen.

Logan looked at his mother. "Don't you believe me, Mom?"

"It's not that we don't believe you. It's just harder for us to understand because we weren't there with you. We don't know anyone who's gone back in time before."

"And we still don't." Dad poured a shot of brandy into his coffee.

Logan's mom appeared to stab at him with her eyes before turning back to Logan. "Can you tell us anything more about the man who took you back in time?"

"Robert? Just what I told you the day I got home. He was the homeless man outside the Chick-Fil-A, and he was an angel."

"So, how did he get into your room?"

"I don't know. I think he came in through the window."

"Is that what he told you?"

"No. I just assumed because the window was open, and he said he was an angel. I guessed he must have flown in."

Dad threw his hand in the air like he was tossing a Frisbee. "Listen to him, Karen. He's talking about angels as if they're real."

"They are real, Dad."

Logan and his mom turned to the sound of a spoon clanging against the kitchen sink.

"That's it," Dad said. "I've heard enough. Logan, you've been home for two days now. It's time to stop this fantasy about seeing Jesus and the angels. Start telling the truth."

"But it *is* the truth, Dad. Honest." Logan felt his throat closing, as if he were about to cry.

"Yeah, just like that story you told two years ago after having your appendix out. Didn't you tell all your friends that the three holes in your belly from the surgery were the result of you having been shot by a robber?"

Logan dropped his chin.

"Or that whopper you told last year about there being a bomb in the basement at school. That one caused a big stir, didn't it? School officials had to evacuate the building. The police were called. And a bomb disposal unit and K-9 search team were dispatched."

"That was different. I was just trying to scare some girls who were picking on me."

"A lie is a lie."

Mom let out a sigh. "Brad."

"No, Karen. This has gone on long enough, and it's hindering the police investigation. Logan, you can just spend the rest of the day in your room. And no TV or video games until you make up your mind to tell us the truth."

"But—"

"No buts. Now go to your room."

Logan's eyes welled with tears. He ran to his

room and slammed the door. Even though his mother hadn't come out and admitted she didn't believe him, he suspected she really didn't. Worse, his stepfather had all but called him a liar, which for him was far worse than having no TV or video games.

* * *

Wendell's bladder felt like it was about to burst. But with less than five minutes to midnight, he wasn't about to leave his spot to search for a place to relieve himself. Not and take a chance on missing the fireworks. Instead, he shifted from foot to foot like a little boy, packed together with the other hundred-thousand-plus sardines gathered at 7th Avenue and Broadway waiting for the New Year.

Wendell had arrived in Times Square just before 4:00 p.m. to secure a prime viewing spot. By 8:00, the crowd had grown so dense he barely had to move to engage in one of his favorite pastimes. With groups of young women surrounding him—all jostling for a better vantage point—he merely had to lean forward to find his nose buried in a head of hair. His only hindrance, the occasional winter hat or piece of celebratory head gear.

A rise in crowd noise signaled the descent of the ball atop the One Times Square building. Wendell's pulse quickened. His mind raced. What if when the ball dropped it set off a huge explosion, one large enough to bring down the building. By the time the ball reached the bottom, he was out of breath.

The crowd erupted into delirium with the changing of the year, followed by the first fireworks displays exploding overhead. Wendell cheered right along with them, only not for the new year, but for the explosions. Several of the girls around him covered their ears, which he found ironic considering they were at a fireworks display. He jumped, pumping his fist in rhythm with the detonations. He was so excited he barely noticed the warmness building in his pants until the urine flowed down his legs.

People hugged and kissed one another all around, including two girls who hugged him. A third started to give him a kiss but stopped short when her face got close to his, opting for a hug instead.

A minute later, a girl kept blowing a horn in his ear, hampering his enjoyment of the explosions. He turned to her. "Get that thing out of my ear. I'm trying to enjoy the fireworks."

The girl scowled. "Well, excuse me. I didn't know they were *your* fireworks."

As soon as Wendell turned back around, the girl put the horn up next to his ear and blew. He whirled to grab it, threw it to the ground, and smashed it.

The girl glared at him with cold eyes. "Who do you think you are anyway?" She cursed at him in a thick Brooklyn accent. She bent to retrieve the horn but rose quickly when she noticed liquid surrounding the instrument and a trail leading to Wendell's feet. She jumped up and pointed at him, laughing. "This guy just peed himself."

The crowd near him backed away, their faces twisted, arms pointing. Many joined the girl in laughing at Wendell. "Somebody get this boy a diaper," a male in the crowd said, which inspired even more laughter.

Wendell wanted to run, as far and a fast as he could. But because of the number of people gathered, the best he could do was to push his way through. *That was stupid, Wendell. If you hadn't said anything, no one would have noticed that you'd peed yourself.* On the way out, he continued to hear the laughs and jeers of the crowd behind him.

Ten minutes later, he was halfway home to his apartment in Chelsea when he reached into his jacket pocket and pulled out a Sprite soda can with sixteen inches of fuse hanging out of the top. It was a package he'd hoped to deliver somewhere closer to the festivities in Times Square that evening, but with all the police security, he didn't dare make the attempt.

Earlier in the week, he'd painstakingly removed the powder from each of the 640 firecrackers in his stash. Using two sets of tweezers, he'd tied the ends of the individual fuses together to make one long string and lowered it into the soda can. He then filled it near the top with the black powder, packed it tight with a layer of kitty litter, and sealed the hole with softened wax.

Now, with his original plan foiled, he needed a secondary target. He turned right from 7th Avenue onto 25th Street and came upon a small church with a half red brick front set overtop a series of beige arched alcoves. The sign on the front read, "St. Columba Catholic Church." He slipped into one of the alcoves hoping to find a window he could break. Unable to locate one, he checked the street one more time before moving to the center alcove and placing his device at the bottom of the main door of the church. He lit the fuse and sprinted east on 25th Street, stopping just before reaching 9th Avenue to bear witness to his handiwork.

Fire, smoke, and pieces of splintered wood poured out from the alcove when the device exploded, the concussion setting off multiple car alarms on the street. Wendell continued away from the scene, reducing his gait to avoid drawing attention to himself before turning right onto 9th Avenue. He walked slowly all the way back to his apartment.

Just before entering the building, the sound of the first sirens entering the neighborhood reached his ears. He smiled, realizing the heavy concentration of police in Times Square probably served to aid his escape. A sense of pride welled in his chest. This was no picket protest, no graffiti scrawled on the rear retaining wall of a church parking lot. This was a direct and violent act perpetrated in furtherance of the atheist doctrine and against the foundations of religious tyranny.

CHAPTER 19

January 1

Marcus responded to a request by Daniel Flores, Assistant Director in Charge of the Manhattan Bureau, to appear in his office. "Come in and sit down, Marcus," AD Flores said when Marcus appeared in his doorway. "How's the Ailshie investigation coming?"

"We're making headway. This morning, Logan and his mother identified our suspect from a photo array as the homeless man they saw on 6th Avenue. And the boy confirmed it was the same man who showed up in his bedroom later that evening."

"I heard there was a problem with your suspect."

"Other than he supposedly died seventy years ago, no problem at all."

"Huh. What are you doing about it?"

"Our examiners identified twenty or more matching points on four of the seven latents lifted from the boy's bedroom during the first and second processing. All belonging to Robert Templeton. The guy who left the prints is definitely the guy whose prints we have on file. We're just not sure the prints we have are Templeton's."

"Then whose are they?"

"The mistake has to have originated with the National Personnel Records Center, which maintains the service records of all military personnel. The records center is a part of the National Archives and Records Administration. Someone with access to Templeton's records may have switched, either accidentally or deliberately, Templeton's prints with someone who is still alive today. We've launched an investigation into that possibility."

"Good. And the lookout?"

"We've issued a nationwide BOLO for Templeton on suspicion of kidnapping." Marcus pulled a report from the folder on his lap.

"Great. Let's make sure we—" Dan leaned forward across his desk and lifted his chin in a half nod. "What do you have there?"

"Lab report on the boy's shirt, jacket, and the copper coin he was carrying."

His eyebrows rose. "Oh."

"DNA analysis shows both clothing items were stained with blood belonging to Logan Ailshie. It also shows they were stained with the saliva of a wolf. And not just any wolf. Genetic testing revealed the species to be an Arabian wolf."

"How is that significant?"

"As the name indicates, Arabian wolves are only found in Arabia. Today their range is limited to a few specific countries, including southern Israel, Jordan, and Saudi Arabia. Two thousand years ago, however, they roamed the entire Arabian Peninsula. So unless Logan visited a zoo that houses an Arabian wolf, his claim to have been bitten by one while in Bethlehem has some merit."

"I thought you said when the boy arrived home,

there wasn't any sign of injury to his shoulder."

Marcus shook his head. He still hadn't reconciled his own encounter with Robert Templeton, and now this. "The skin in that area was absolutely pristine. And no evidence of scabbing or scarring."

Dan frowned. "What do you think happened to him?"

"I don't know yet. But the analysis of the coin is equally intriguing. Based on the stamped markings found on the coin, it appears to be a mite. How much do you know about the Bible?"

"Not much."

"Me neither, so I had to look it up. It's the denomination mentioned in the Gospels of Mark and Luke in the story of the widow's mites. Voltammetric electroanalytical dating indicates the boy's coin was minted some time before Jesus' birth."

"Aren't there a considerable number of these coins still in circulation today?"

"Sure, but when taken in light of the other evidence we've uncovered, I believe it adds a shred of credibility to the boy's story."

Dan folded his hands on the desk and tilted his head. "Marcus, please tell me you're not swallowing what the kid told you about getting the coin from Joseph himself?"

Marcus chuckled. "No, I'm not ready to take a bite out of that sandwich just yet."

"Good. Because none of what you've shown me here today could hardly be considered conclusive." He reached for his earlobe. "Look, my money's on a mix-up at the National Archives. That, and the probability the boy is either delusional or acting out a fantasy."

Leaning in, Marcus peered directly into his boss's eyes. "Dan, I know this kid has a creative imagination, but except for the religious fantasy element, everything he's told us about Templeton has been corroborated by the physical evidence. I'd like to at least follow through with that aspect of the case."

Dan nodded slowly. "All right. Stay with the lookout and let me know what happens with the NPRC investigation. But my feeling from talking to the director is he'd like to get this thing wrapped up as quickly as possible. We've already expended more resources than we can justify for a case without a prosecutable crime."

"What about the kidnapping?"

"Didn't you tell me the boy said he went with Templeton voluntarily?"

"Yeah, but how voluntary can the will of a nine-year-old boy be?"

"A valid point, but without evidence that Templeton intended to hurt him or ask for a ransom, you'll never get a conviction in court for kidnapping. Especially if Logan decides to testify in Templeton's defense."

Dan was right. Without a clear criminal motive, they'd never obtain a conviction for kidnapping of Templeton or anyone else. Then again, motive wasn't Marcus's chief concern at the moment. Logan's disappearance and return constituted a mystery, one he was determined to get to the bottom of regardless of the why. Besides, Marcus had another piece of evidence his colleagues weren't privy to — the possible connection of his friend from the cemetery.

* * *

A day later, Logan led Florence Simonetti, a child psychologist with Manhattan Psychology Group, through a door leading to an outer-office seating area where his parents waited. They rose quickly to greet them.

"All done?" Mom said.

"All done," Logan said, "Dr. Flo says I'm going to be fine."

"That's wonderful, dear. But you should really address her as Dr. Simonetti."

"No, Mom, she told me to call her Dr. Flo."

Logan's mom smiled at the doctor. "All right. Why don't you sit here for a few minutes while your father and I have a word with her?"

"No problem," he said, flopping into a chair and picking up a copy of *Highlights* magazine from the table. He loved exploring the seek and find section of hidden objects puzzles.

His parents met with Dr. Flo on the opposite side of the room near the door. "Doctor," Dad whispered, "what's the verdict?"

Pretending to read the magazine, Logan giggled inside. He never understood how adults believed that if they whispered, their conversations wouldn't be overheard. As for Dr. Flo, she was younger than he'd expected, in her thirties, although her short blonde hair and glasses made her look scholarly enough.

"First, I want to say that in my seventeen years as a child psychologist, I have never heard a more detailed and engaging story from a patient like the one told by your son. If I didn't know better, I would've thought he'd really experienced it."

"What does that mean?" Mom said.

"Unfortunately, it means your son is probably suffering from something we call delusional disorder."

Logan looked up in time to see his mother drop her head. "Dear Lord," she said.

Dr. Flo put her hand on Mom's shoulder. "It's not as bad as it sounds. As far as psychiatric disorders go, delusional disorder is one of the least serious in the group of diagnoses we call the schizophrenia spectrum. Patients with delusional disorder don't normally suffer from odd behaviors otherwise associated with the classic symptoms of schizophrenia — hallucinations, thought disorder, mood swings. I certainly didn't see any evidence of those when speaking with Logan. And I interviewed him for over three hours."

"Are you sure, doctor?" Mom said. "Couldn't it just be a fantasy?"

Dr. Flo shook her head. "Fantasies originate in the imagination and can usually be overcome by the introduction of evidence contradicting the fantasy. A delusion is a strongly held conviction of a false belief, one that is highly resistant to the existence of factual evidence. In Logan's case, he absolutely believes an angel named Robert took him back in time to witness the birth of Christ, and that his injured shoulder was healed by the touch of Jesus."

Dad touched his chin while addressing the doctor. "What's the treatment for this delusional disorder."

"Studies have shown a combination of psychotherapy and medication have proven to be the most effective method. I'd like to begin by scheduling a series of individual psychotherapeutic counseling sessions with your son. Later, depending on how Logan responds, we may want to transition to counseling in a family setting."

Logan's chest tightened. *Oh, great. The first steps toward putting me in a looney bin.*

"I'd also like to try putting him on a low dose of Risperidone and see how he does."

"Is it dangerous?" his mom said.

"Not at all, especially when prescribed in a lower dose. Risperidone is one of a group of antipsychotic drugs that block the reception of dopamine and serotonin in the brain, the two neurotransmitters believed responsible for the development of delusions."

Logan dropped the magazine onto the table, leaned back in the chair and crossed his arms. He'd watched enough TV to know people prescribed antipsychotic drugs often walked around like the walking dead. He didn't want any part of it.

He watched the three of them move to the receptionist's window to schedule Logan's first appointment. Dr. Flo wrote out a prescription on a pad and handed it to his mother. *How do I get out of this one?*

Logan didn't say much through dinner, still fuming at the prospect of being drugged for telling the truth. But by allowing his parents to carry the table conversation, he hoped to divert attention from himself long enough so they'd forget about him. Normally, when he had medicine to take, they'd give it to him just before or immediately following a meal. In this case, he'd anticipated having a day or two of grace before starting the medication, but Dad insisted they stop at the pharmacy on the way home.

"May I be excused?" he said.

"Before dessert?" Mom said, "we're having lemon meringue pie."

Refusing dessert. That should work. If they think I'm not feeling well, maybe they'll skip trying to drug him. "No thanks, I think I'll just go to my room."

As he got up from the table Dad shook a fork at him. "Don't forget. No TV or video games."

"Yes, sir."

He made it to his bedroom door before his mom called to him. He turned to see her coming toward him with a pill in one hand and his unfinished glass of milk in the other. "Now's a good time to start your medication." She opened her palm.

Logan felt a sort of pressure close in on him from all sides. He looked at the pill like it was a rattlesnake about to bite him. "I'm not taking that."

"Why? It's completely safe."

"Because I'm not crazy."

"Honey, nobody's saying you're crazy."

"Oh, really? I overheard what you guys were talking about with Dr. Flo. She says I have a delusion. That's the same as being called crazy."

"That's only because the story you told her is difficult to fathom. Like I told you the other day, we don't know anyone who's gone back in time before. And I'm sure she doesn't either."

"And what about all those things you used to teach me about Jesus from the Bible. Don't you believe them?"

Dad cleared his throat, which drew an immediate frown his mother.

"Of course I do, Logan. But all those things I taught you happened thousands of years ago, not during the last nine days you were away from us. Do you understand?"

Logan lowered his eyes. No, he didn't understand. Didn't understand why his own parents wouldn't accept what he'd seen was real. And because he couldn't convince them, they were going to force him to take a drug he didn't want or need.

Dad stood from the table and joined them. "I still say it was a dream." He smiled and put his hand on Logan's shoulder. "I think after a few days of taking your medication, you'll come to realize that's all it was. Just a dream."

Mom held out her palm again. "It's okay."

Tears filled Logan's eyes. "Please don't make me take it."

Dad's face softened. He nodded at Mom, and she withdrew her hand. "All right. Why don't you just go ahead to your room? Your mother and I will talk about it and decide what to do. Maybe Dr. Flo will agree to begin treatment with just the therapy sessions."

Sobbing, Logan entered his room. Robert had warned him there'd be people who wouldn't believe his story, but he never thought they would include his parents.

CHAPTER 20

Wendell never dreamed he'd find something on the internet to excite him more than watching dirty movies. But as he began to type the names of various bombs and bomb-making materials into the search engine of his computer, he felt his pulse quicken.

During the four days following the detonation of his homemade M-80, he'd listened to every television and radio broadcast and read every newspaper looking for a story about his accomplishment. There'd been a small item on the back pages of two of the newspapers about a destruction to the outside of the St. Columba church. But since there hadn't been any injuries and no group claimed responsibility, it didn't receive any follow-up attention.

Inspired by the attention and his reading of the McVeigh and Kaczynski biographies, Wendell hoped to learn all there was to learn about explosives. Despite the less than dramatic results of his first experiment, he loved the feeling of power it gave him. And he wanted more.

Wendell's first search brought up a list of twenty-eight conventional bombs on Wikipedia alone. And he reviewed every one of them. Following over eleven hours of research, in which he ate nothing and took only a single bathroom break, he narrowed his choices to three. He printed out everything he could find on how to make a pipe bomb, a pressure cooker bomb, and a homemade ANFO or fertilizer bomb. Each was chosen for the same reason — they were easy to construct from readily available materials.

He loved the simplicity and easy-to-conceal nature of the pipe bomb but was wary of the risks of premature detonation, which appeared common. The pressure cooker bomb, used successfully by both the Boston Marathon and Chelsea bombers, could be packed with more explosives than the pipe bomb, yet remain easily transportable. The fertilizer bomb, depending on the size of the container chosen, had the advantage of producing the largest explosion, but at the expense of both concealability and transportability.

Beyond his choice of a device, Wendell also contemplated the selection of his next objective. He wasn't only looking to make a bigger bomb. He wanted a more important target, one that would serve as an example to his fellow atheists of the need for more decisive action in their war against Christianity. What about CNC Headquarters? Their hosts were always interviewing some nationally recognized priest or pastor, or highlighting some screwy faith-based cause.

Though he'd only been working there for a day, his supervisor, Mort Childress, had given him the fifteen-cent tour of the facility, including all eight CNC broadcast studios. Through the entire tour, Wendell behaved like a kid making his first visit to Disney World. From the famous arched couch of Studio 6, to the numerous video walls surrounding Studio 10, to the Starship Enterprise bridge-like layout of Studio 9,

Wendell remained in awe.

Of course, as a part of two three-person cleaning crews, each assigned to clean four of the studios a night, he'd get the opportunity to work them all. Mr. Childress posted a weekly schedule designating which crew was assigned to what group of studios on a rotating basis. Tonight, and in the coming nights, Wendell would attempt to explore some of the studios more thoroughly to identify any potential hiding places for his next bomb.

* * *

At 6:12 a.m. on January 5th, the phone rang in the living room of the Thompson residence. After the fourth call, Logan gave up trying to sleep and rolled out of bed. He came out of his room rubbing his eyes. Mom had the phone cradled against her ear, and Dad stood next to the couch sipping a cup of coffee.

"What's with all the phone calls this morning," Logan said.

Dad put a finger to his lips. "That's what your mother's trying to find out now."

She covered the receiver. "It's Colleen. She says Logan is on the front page of every newspaper in town."

Colleen Swanson, a redheaded mother of four from Queens, was Mom's best friend.

Dad looked down at the flashing light on the answering machine. "So that's why the media's been calling here all morning. What happened?"

"Someone leaked the statement Logan gave to the authorities, including everything he said about traveling back in time to witness the birth of Jesus."

She returned her attention to the call for another few seconds. "Oh, my goodness."

"What is it, Karen?"

"She pointed to the front door. "Get the paper."

Dad spilled coffee on the table before hurrying to the front door.

"All right, Colleen. I will. Brad just brought in the paper. We'll take a look. Thanks for calling." After she hung up the phone, she met Logan and his stepdad in the kitchen.

Dad spread *The New York Times* on the kitchen table so they could read it together. He paused to curse halfway through the article, something he rarely did in front of Logan.

"Brad, please," Mom said.

"Lousy FBI. Victims' statements are supposed to remain confidential."

"Agent Garraway?" she said, her voice rising. "I don't believe it. He'd never do such a thing."

"Oh, he wouldn't, would he? Who else had a copy of Logan's statement?"

They continued reading. A minute later, she looked up. "Brad, this article is suggesting that Logan's disappearance was a hoax and is calling for the FBI to drop the investigation entirely. If Garraway or someone else at the FBI is behind the release, why would they leak a statement that made themselves look bad?"

Dad furrowed his brow. "You're right. Why would they?"

Logan took several more minutes to examine the article, his eyes misting over by the time he'd finished. "Oh, man. This makes it sound like I'm crazy *and* a liar."

Mom put her arm around him. "Try not to let it upset you. One of the things we've learned from living in this city is that the media is more interested in sensationalism than in reporting the facts."

"It's because they don't believe me. They think I'm delusional, just like Dr. Flo." Logan put his finger on a paragraph of the article. "It says right here that one of the reasons the authorities haven't been able to solve the case is because of the fantastic nature of my story."

"That doesn't necessarily mean—"

"They also say I have a long history of storytelling, including that thing with the bomb at school." He moved his finger to another paragraph. "And look here, some are even calling me The Boy Who Cried Wolf."

"Sweetheart—"

He stepped out of his mother's embrace. "No, Mom. The don't believe me about Robert, about the angels, or Jesus. None of it." He crossed his arms. "But I know what I saw."

"Too bad we don't have any proof to back it up," Dad said.

"You want proof." Logan unbuttoned his pajama top and exposed his right shoulder. "Take a look at where the wolf bit me on the shoulder."

Brad examined the boy's shoulder again. "I still don't see anything."

"That's because Jesus healed it when he grabbed my finger."

"I know, you told us. Unfortunately, your word alone isn't proof."

"Then how about this." Logan stood, took off his pajama top, and pulled down the waist of his pajama bottom to expose his stomach. "What happened to the scars from my appendix surgery?"

Dad walked around the table for a closer look.

"I had three of them. One here, here, and here." Logan pointed to the three incision areas across his stomach. "You and Mom saw them. Now they're gone."

His mother knelt beside him and lightly brushed her fingertips across the area where the incisions had been made. "When did you notice they weren't there anymore?"

"A day or two after we returned from seeing Jesus."

"After He touched you?"

"Yes."

His mother lifted wide eyes to his dad.

"Don't give me that look, Karen. I'm sure there's a logical explanation."

"And what might that be?"

Dad tilted his head and scratched his temple. "Give me a minute. I'll think of one."

"How about this? A year after his operation, another surgical team snuck in here while we were asleep and performed plastic surgery to remove the scars."

"Ha-ha."

"Sorry, but that's the only logical explanation I can come up with. I have a spiritual one, but you already know what that is."

"That Jesus did it?"

"Why not?"

"I like your other explanation better."

A disturbance outside drew their attention to the front of the building, and they moved to the living room window. Dozens of reporters and a half dozen media trucks lined the street and sidewalk below. Dad shook his head. "Will you look at those vultures? We won't be able to leave the apartment without a military escort. That, or we'll have to put on disguises and leave by the service entrance."

Logan's mother snorted. "And we thought the nightmare was over." She picked up Logan's pajama top and handed it to him. "We were thinking about letting you go back to school tomorrow, but with all this going on maybe it's not such a good idea."

"Oh, no, Mom. I want to go back to school. I miss my friends."

* * *

Marcus marched into AD Flores's office and dropped a copy of the morning newspaper on his desk. "Somebody just made our job a whole lot harder," he said.

Dan took a minute to scan the article, then cursed before looking up at Marcus. "What knucklehead's responsible for this?"

"I don't know for sure, but it has to be somebody within the agency. Nobody else had access to the statement."

Dan returned to reading the newspaper for another minute before slapping at it with the back of his hand. "Will you look at this. Whoever leaked this conveniently left out the fact we had forensic evidence linking a possible suspect to the crime scene."

"Which makes it look like we're conducting a full-scale investigation based solely on a boy's fantasy. No wonder they're calling for us to drop the case."

Dan shook his head. "And I thought those days were behind us."

"What days?"

"Here we are, the premiere law enforcement agency in America, and we can't maintain security over one kid's statement. This place leaks worse than the oil pan on a thirty-eight Ford. Not that we should be surprised, given the example set by our former director."

The stain of that betrayal was still fresh in every FBI employee's mind and had changed forever the public's perception that the bureau was an independent, non-partisan agency. "Yeah, but his motives were purely political. What do you think our leaker's aim is?"

"It's hard to say. It's not a strong case to begin with, so what this person hopes to gain by leaking it to the press is beyond me. Where are we on the NPRC investigation?"

"You would have to ask that question." Marcus pulled a chair in front of Dan's desk and sat. "We interviewed everyone—everyone still living, that is—who had access to Templeton's service records. Nothing. Then we obtained a copy of the original military fingerprint card and compared it to his 1942 War Department Identification, which, again, we obtained from Private Templeton's grandniece."

Dan's mouth fell open. "Don't tell me. The fingerprints on the two cards match."

"Not only do the prints match, but also the signatures, according to our handwriting expert."

"We're still looking for a dead man?"

"Exactly."

"I still say there's a rational explanation for all this. I don't know what it is right now, but hopefully we'll find out when this guy turns up as a result of the BOLO. In the meantime, I want this leaker's hide, preferably peeled from their body in one-inch strips a piece at a time."

"You want a formal inquiry?"

"You better believe it—interviews, polygraphs, the works."

"Who do you want to do the investigation, OIG?"

"Nah, our Internal Investigations Section should be able to handle it. And Marcus," Dan steadied his gaze at him, "I sure hope none of your people are involved, but if they are."

"I understand."

"Who was the primary transcriber on the boy's statement?"

"Vivian Scofield."

"Let's make sure they start with her."

CHAPTER 21

The following afternoon, Logan sat outside the principal's office at school playing with his iPhone while waiting for his mom to arrive. His morning had been eventful, to say the least.

Despite waking up feeling groggy for a second straight day, he insisted on going to school. When he entered his classroom, he approached Ms. Davis, his fourth-grade teacher, at her desk to ask permission to share his story with the class. She denied the request, citing a school policy that prohibits engaging in religious activities on school property. Nevertheless, during the morning he received several requests from classmates who'd heard the news and wanted to know the details of his ordeal.

During lunch, Logan recited his story to the collection of students seated at his long, bench-style table in the cafeteria. As other children finished their lunch, they joined the group, either by squeezing into the benches or standing behind those that did. Logan found himself surrounded by over fifty students.

When the school bell rang signaling the end of lunch, most of the students filed out of the cafeteria to their next class. But while Logan continued to speak, not a single student moved from around his table, their bodies seemingly frozen in place. Several of the departing students hurled insults at them, which drew several scowls and at least one jeer from those listening to Logan's story. He talked through the second bell.

Ten minutes later, the principal, Margaret Thornburg, a middle-aged woman dressed in a gray tweed suit and red blouse entered the cafeteria. She ordered the students to their classes before escorting Logan to the office.

Now, Logan's mom entered the principal's office and sat next to him. "What's this all about? What happened?"

Logan pointed behind her to an approaching Mrs. Thornburg. "Ask her."

"Good afternoon, Mrs. Thomas," the administrator said. "I'm sorry to have to call you down here like this, but Logan caused a disturbance in the cafeteria today."

"What kind of disturbance?"

"He was preventing other students from returning to their regularly scheduled afternoon classes."

Logan's mother straightened herself in her chair. "And just how was he doing that? Did he have a gun to their head, or something?"

Mrs. Thomas pursed her lips, shaking her head slightly. "Nothing like that. But by sharing with the students the details of his imagined trip back in time, he captivated them to the point where they ignored the after lunch bell."

"Okay, I still don't see where my son did anything wrong."

"Mrs. Thomas, school policy prohibits in the engaging of religious activities or proselytizing on school property, or in *any* activity that serves as a disruption to others from doing their work. You see, even looking at it in the broadest terms, Logan's behavior would be considered both religious and disruptive."

Logan's mother turned to him.

"I was just doing what Robert told me to do, Mom. Telling what I saw."

Mrs. Thornburg put a hand to her chin. "This Robert is the angel who supposedly took your son back in time?"

"Yes, but how did you know?"

"I read the newspaper. I'm also sorry to have to tell you that we're going to have to suspend your son from school for the next seven days."

His mother looked dazed. "But he just came back today."

"I know, and I feel terrible about that, believe me. But the news about this incident is already all over the school. How long do you think it will take for the ACLU to get wind of it? We just can't take the chance of their filing a lawsuit."

Logan's mom stood and let out a big sigh. "All right. Let's go home."

Mrs. Thornburg leaned into his mother's ear. "In the meantime, you may want to take him to see a child psychologist."

"Too late. They already did," Logan said, stomping toward the office door. *Why are adults so predictable?*

* * *

"That was fast," AD Flores leaned back in his office chair. "Less than two days. It was the Scofield woman after all?"

Seated again in front of his desk, Marcus pointed a finger at his boss. "You called it, Dan. She cracked quicker than a cold egg dropped into boiling water. They didn't even have to polygraph her."

"And her motive?"

"Believe it or not, she says she didn't do it to harm the bureau. Evidently, she's a dyed-in-the-wool atheist. Very active in one of the local chapters."

"Oh, great. A zealot."

"She said she leaked the statement in an effort to damage Christianity by mocking the idea of Christmas itself. She believed by releasing the details of Logan's absurd story, it would serve to discredit the very notion of the birth of a Savior. She thought it was especially important to get the word out just after the Christmas season, while it was still fresh in people's minds."

"Like I said, a zealot. How in the world did we ever hire someone like her?"

"Unfortunately, they don't wear signs. And even if they did, nondiscrimination policies would prevent us from disqualifying them."

"I'm glad you brought that up. We'll have to ensure there's no mention of her religious leanings in the press release. As far as the public is concerned, she was just another employee terminated for violating bureau policy."

"The director's already made that call?"

"Got off the phone with him not two minutes before you came in. We were discussing what to put in the bulletin . . . including the fact that we're suspending the investigation."

Marcus jerked his head back slightly. "Suspending

the—"

"Pending apprehension of the suspect, Robert Templeton, or the person posing as him."

"Why now?"

"Several reasons, the first we discussed the other day. Money. We're spending too much of it on a case that in all likelihood will never be prosecuted. The second is practicality, since the boy has already been safely returned to his family."

"Anything else?"

"Yes, and the one of most concern to the director. Our reputation. Since the press got hold of the boy's statement, we've been taking a public relations beating. They question the wisdom of our spending taxpayer money on such an obvious hoax. Just the other day, the director said he overheard someone refer to us as the Fantasy Bureau of Investigation."

"What did he say about Templeton?"

"What could he say? We can't tell the public we're looking for a guy whose been dead for over seventy years. If they thought we were fools for believing a kid's story about going back in time, they'd really start calling for us to be fitted for straightjackets with that one."

"But what about—"

"Relax, Marcus. You've still got your BOLO. If this guy shows up, we can always reopen the investigation. But for now, it's a dead issue."

Marcus slumped back in the chair.

"You look like someone just took your birthday away. What is it?"

Marcus shrugged.

Dan's eyes widened. "No . . . no, you're not."

"Not what?"

"You not starting to believe the kid, are you?"

"It's not that. I want to make sure we're not overlooking anything, no matter how bizarre."

"Bizarre is right. This case has been a three-headed orangutan from the start. It's time to move on."

But Marcus couldn't move on, not without knowing the truth. And yes, he was starting to believe Logan's story. There was just too much evidence not to anymore. And with the bureau pulling the plug on the investigation, his only hope of getting to the truth now was to locate Robert Templeton.

CHAPTER 22

Marcus checked his watch to make sure it was past 9 p.m. before approaching the Thomases's apartment. Surely Logan would be asleep by now. Concerned about the reception he might receive, he rang their doorbell and took a step back from the threshold.

Mr. Thomas opened the door and seeing him, put a hand on his hip and shook his head. "I didn't think you'd have the guts to show your face at this door again. Karen, look who's here. It's Agent Garraway."

Mrs. Thomas walked toward them from the kitchen. "Don't leave him standing out in the hallway. Ask him to come in."

Mr. Thomas opened the door wider, throwing his left arm out toward the center of the room in an exaggerated gesture of welcome. "Why not?"

Marcus moved through the foyer to the living room. "I apologize for not calling ahead first, but I was afraid you wouldn't see me."

"You have good instincts," Mr. Thomas said. "Why are you here? You stop by to get more information for your next press release?"

"Brad." Mrs. Thomas focused on Agent Garraway. "I'd like to apologize for my husband. We've all been under a lot of stress lately."

"Stress. Are you kidding? Do you have any idea what our son — no, what we've all been through? Just listen to this." He played back the first three messages on the answering machine. The first one suggested they have Logan committed to a mental institution, or better yet, put down like a rabid dog. The second consisted of a series of vile and vulgar taunts interlaced with curse words. The third suggested Logan prove he was an angel by throwing himself out the window of their apartment. "And that's just a sample of the harassment we've received since you guys leaked the statement."

Mrs. Thomas pointed to the chair closest to Marcus. "Please sit down, Agent Garraway."

Marcus sat and folded his hands. "I can't tell you how sorry I am about the statement, and more than that, about how its release has affected your family. But I can assure you none of the investigators assigned to your son's case were responsible."

"Then who was it?" Mr. Thomas said.

"A member of our secretarial staff who worked on transcribing the statement. Her employment with the bureau has been terminated."

Mr. Thomas's bearing softened. He let out a huge breath. "Thanks for telling us. For a while there we thought we might lose confidence in the FBI."

"And I hope you still don't after I've finished. Apologizing for the leak was only part of the reason for my coming here tonight."

"And the other part?"

"To tell you I believe the story your son told us."

"Yeah, well, we assumed *that* when you stopped looking at Karen and me as suspects."

"I don't think you understand. What I mean is that

I believe his *whole* story, including the part about his going back in time to see Jesus."

Mr. Thomas's mouth dropped open, but his wife just smiled. "You're joking," he said.

"I know this must sound strange, a federal agent admitting his belief in miracles, but the fact is there's too much evidence to conclude otherwise."

"What evidence?" Mr. Thomas said.

"The lab found two substances on your son's clothing, his blood, and the saliva of an Arabian wolf. Arabian wolves are only found in the Middle East."

"How can that be?" Mr. Thomas said. "There wasn't a scratch on his shoulder."

"I can't explain it. I'm just telling you what the serological tests show."

With a dazed look on his face, Mr. Thomas lowered himself into the other chair next to his wife.

"There's more," Marcus said. "The tests we ran on the coin Logan said he got from Joseph indicates it originated during the time of Christ."

"That doesn't prove he actually got it from Joseph," Mr. Thomas said.

Marcus gave a half shrug. "No, but—"

Mrs. Thomas leaned forward in her chair "Should we tell Agent Garraway what Logan showed us the other morning?"

"Oh for—" Mr. Thomas took the Lord's name in vain. "—Karen. What do you want to do that for?"

"When Logan was seven, we rushed him to the hospital for an emergency appendectomy. Fortunately, the doctors were able to perform the surgery laparoscopically, although the procedure left three distinct scars on his abdomen. A few days ago, Logan showed us his stomach. The scars had completely disappeared, without any evidence they'd ever been there. He said Jesus healed them in the same way he healed his shoulder after the wolf attacked him."

"By touching his finger?"

"Yes," she said.

Mr. Thomas crossed his arms. "Okay, I'll admit all this stuff about Logan's unexplained healing and his possession of an ancient coin is intriguing. But there's still no way you're going to get me to buy into his traveling back in time."

"I'm sure a lot of people expressed similar doubts about man being able to fly, to land on the moon, or to complete a successful heart transplant." Marcus waved his hand next to his ear. "I know. I know. It all sounds crazy. And normally, I'm the most skeptical, pragmatic man on the face of the earth. But in this case . . . well, the evidence speaks for itself."

Mr. Thomas folded his hands in front of him. "All right, you say you believe Logan. I accept that. What about your superiors at the bureau?"

"Unfortunately, they're required to concern themselves with things beyond the existence of facts, like appearances, politics. Which brings me to the third reason for my visit this evening. The FBI is suspending further active investigation of your son's case."

Mrs. Thomas placed fingers to her parting lips. "Can I ask why?"

"A host of reasons, really, but they all boil down to one thing: Your son's story just isn't believable . . . to everyone other than me, that is."

"What about Logan's disappearance for seven days?" Mr. Thomas said. "Surely you don't find that aspect of the case implausible?"

"No, no we don't. And it's why the nationwide lookout for the person your son identified as Robert will remain in the system."

"Still, you're ending the investigation?" Mrs. Thomas said.

"For all intents and purposes, yes."

Mr. Thomas reached for his wife's hand. "They have to, honey. Actually, I'm surprised they kept it open this long, considering what they had to work with."

Marcus rose from his chair and started for the front door, then paused and turned back to face the Thomases. *Don't do it, Marcus.* "Of course, that doesn't mean you have to accept *their* determination."

"What do you mean?" Mrs. Thomas said.

"It means if you have faith in your son, there's a way for you to keep fighting for the truth."

A sparkle returned to Mrs. Thompson's eyes. "How?"

"Go on the offensive. Turn your enemies' weapons against them. I take it you've been contacted by reporters wanting to tell Logan's story?"

"More than twenty," she said. "A couple of the tabloids have even offered us money."

"I hope you're not considering trusting any of those sharks."

"Not on your life."

"Good. They're only interested in ratings and circulation. And in this town that means attacking anyone who doesn't hold with their liberal views. A story like this, one with strong Christian elements, makes for a particularly juicy target." Marcus reached into his wallet and pulled out a business card, addressing Mrs. Thomas. "If I remember correctly, you're the Christian in the family?"

She took the card from his hand.

"Laurin Greene is a reporter with CNC who covers a lot of their religious news stories. She interviewed me a few years ago during the height of the Catholic priest sex scandal. She's a Christian and a straight shooter."

Mr. Thomas peeked over his wife's shoulder, then reached across and took the card from her. "Aren't we only asking for more trouble by contacting a reporter? Look what happened when that woman leaked Logan's statement. He's become the laughing stock of the city."

"Don't you see, talking to Laurin will give you a chance to set the record straight? And take it from someone who's interviewed your son, he's going to make an impressive witness."

Mr. Thomas shook his head. "I don't think so." He handed the card back to Marcus.

When he did, Mrs. Thomas made strong eye contact with Marcus, and appeared to signal to him with a subtle nod of the head.

"We appreciate the offer," Mr. Thomas said. "But I think the last thing we need right now is more publicity."

Mrs. Thomas walked Agent Garraway to the front door, where he slipped the card into her palm before leaving.

CHAPTER 23

Two days later, as Logan and his mother drove south on 5th Avenue, the boy sat quietly in the front passenger's seat of their Mercedes C300. The pressing of his mother's lips together into a thin line and her two-handed grip of the steering wheel told him she was still upset. His parents had engaged in a fierce argument before his stepfather left for work this morning. They quarreled so loudly that he didn't even have to crack his bedroom door the way he often did when he wanted to eavesdrop on their conversation.

Although Logan hadn't understood all of it, Dad had accused Mom of wanting to go behind his back to secure an interview of their son by a reporter. Dad said he thought they'd agreed last night not to conduct the interview, and it was wrong for her to keep feeding Logan's fantasy. He ended the conversation with "He's your son, you do what you want," before slamming the apartment door on the way out.

Logan had felt his throat tighten. Yet another reminder that the man he called "Dad" didn't really consider himself to be his father. Funny. He couldn't imagine Simeon ever making such a statement.

After his mother parked the car, she and Logan entered the lobby of the CNC Headquarters building.

A brown-skinned lady in a red business dress stood with her back to them talking with a man seated at the front desk. "Excuse me," Mom said. "Are you Ms. Greene?"

The woman pivoted. "Karen Thomas?" They shook hands.

"This is my son —"

"I think I know who this is." Ms. Greene focused on Logan. "I'm so pleased to meet you."

Logan's eyes grew wide. "Gosh, Mom. She's pretty."

His mother chuckled.

Ms. Greene pointed toward a hallway and extended her arm. "Shall we go someplace where you'll be more comfortable?" She led them down the hallway into a room with several tables and a dozen or more fabric covered chairs. She gestured to one of the tables. "Please have a seat." She pulled a chair over so she could face Logan. "Before we get started, I want to say what an incredibly brave young man you are."

Logan blushed. "Thank you."

Ms. Greene addressed his mother. "I also want you to know how much empathy we have for what you and your husband have been through. It's every parent's worst nightmare."

Mom nodded. "I know you touched briefly on this when we spoke this morning, but I still don't understand why you think it's so important to tell Logan's story."

"Two reasons, one practical, the other spiritual."

A grin took over his mother's face.

"I don't need to tell you how adversely your family's been impacted by having your son's story leaked to the media. The negative press coverage, the phone calls, Logan's having been suspended from school. The thing is, the public is being adversely impacted as well because it's not getting the truth."

"And the spiritual reason?" his mom said.

Ms. Greene leaned toward his mother. "As a Christian, I'm sure you've noticed the ever-increasing commercialization of the Christmas holiday over the years. Today, many people more closely associate Santa Claus with Christmas than they do the infant Jesus."

Logan's eyes lit up. "My Mom told me that last week. She said Santa Claus made a better spokesman than Jesus."

"As unfortunate as it is, Logan, your mother is right. Santa Claus does make a better spokesman, at least for things like automobiles, toys, and soft drinks." She shifted her focus to his mom. "And this is where your son comes in. He has a chance to reverse the trend of commercialization, to refocus the public's eye on the true meaning of Christmas, the birth of Jesus Christ."

"Reverse more than a hundred years of established tradition?" Mom said. "A nine-year-old? How?"

"By allowing me to help him tell his story. Your son is the only living witness to an event that took place over two thousand years ago. An event, until now, people could only read about in the Bible."

"You really think it's that important?"

"Mrs. Thomas, your boy has a unique opportunity to not only be a witness for Christ, but also an *eyewitness* for Him. God chose Logan, above all other people on earth, to bring back this message of hope. It would be a crime not to share it with the world."

"Please, Mom," Logan said. "Let me tell my story."

His mother traded glances between Ms. Greene and him. "Let's go for it."

"Great," Ms. Greene said. "If it's all right with you, I'd like to set it up for a week from this Sunday. That'll give us time to advertise. And I want to do it live and in primetime."

"Do you really think Logan can handle a live interview?"

"From what Agent Garraway told me, he'll do great."

Confidence and pride swelled in Logan. He also believed this was his first real opportunity to carry out the mission God had given him.

* * *

The following day, Wendell occupied his usual seat in the front row of the latest meeting of the Manhattan Atheists Association. Tonight, eighteen people. To his surprise, no one chose to sit next to him. A burst of applause signaled the entrance of Terrance Fishburn into the room, who made his way to the podium.

After welcoming the membership, the president began by touting the success of the transit bus system advertising campaign. He advised they'd received a great deal of positive feedback from people who'd seen the signs and voiced appreciation for their anti-religious sentiment. He then thanked the many volunteers who'd worked on the Christmas campaign, citing increases in telephone contributions, pamphlets distributed, and media coverage of picketing efforts.

Mr. Fishburn grasped either side of the podium. "There are, however, two individuals I'd like to call out for special recognition. Two people who put their principles, and the principles of this organization, above their own personal well-being. Wendell Schlump, would you please stand?"

Wendell had no idea what was coming but slowly rose from his seat.

"Ladies and gentlemen. On Christmas Eve, Wendell was arrested and forced to spend the night in jail after being provoked into a fight by one of the actors at a live Nativity scene."

A hearty round of applause erupted from the gathering.

"Way to go, Wendell," a man said.

An elderly gentlemen added, "That's taking one for the team, my boy."

Wendell flushed. He'd never received an applause before, not in his entire life. He turned around, gave a short wave, and returned to his seat.

Mr. Fishburn pointed at him. "Thank you, Wendell, for your sacrifice. Next, I'd like to acknowledge a lady who sacrificed not just her freedom, but her livelihood. Vivian Scofield, would you please rise and be recognized?"

She stood.

This time, the crowd didn't wait for Fishburn to recount her accomplishment, immediately breaking into both cheering and clapping. Several people even gave her a standing ovation.

"I can tell by the response most of you already know of Vivian's act of bravery," Mr. Fishburn said. "But for those of you who may have missed it, Vivian was fired from her job as a secretary with the FBI. And why? Because she had the courage to inform the public that some brat was using a religious fantasy to mislead the FBI into investigating his disappearance. She shouldn't have been fired. She should be promoted."

The volume of cheering and clapping increased. One by one, more people joined the standing chorus of praise until, finally, the entire room was on its feet.

One man cursed. " — the FBI. Nothing but a collection of cheap suits."

"We love you, Vivian," a woman shouted.

Mr. Fishburn raised his hand to quiet the crowd. "Vivian. Hopefully, you can tell by this show of support from our membership how much your devotion to our ideals is appreciated. But in case there's any doubt, I'd like to ask you to please join me at the podium."

When Vivian met Mr. Fishburn at the front of the room, he pulled out what appeared to be a check and handed it to her. "As president of the Manhattan Atheists Association, I'd like to present you with this check in the amount of three-thousand dollars to help with expenses while you look for another job."

Another round of applause ensued. Tears welled Ms. Scofield's eyes, eventually to the point where she had to wipe at one of the corners with her fingers. When the show of appreciation died down, she slowly scanned the crowd. "I don't know how to thank you all for your generosity and support. It's good to know during times like these there are people out there who share your same values. But I'd be less than honest if I didn't tell you I may have made a terrible mistake."

Whispered rumblings ran through the congregation. "What mistake?" a young man near the back said.

"My goal in releasing the boy's statement was to discredit the boy's lie by letting the world see how preposterous his story was. And up until now, my strategy appears to be working. The boy and his story about going back in time to see Jesus have been universally ridiculed in the press."

"I don't quite follow you," Mr. Fishburn said. "How did you make a mistake?"

"Just before leaving to come here tonight, I saw a commercial for a television special appearing on CNC next Sunday. They're planning to do a live interview of Logan Ailshie in prime time.

More rumblings rose from the crowd.

"As most of you know, CNC has a large following among conservatives and some independents. My fear is in putting a fundamentalist spin on the boy's story, they may succeed in undoing the damage caused by my leaking the statement. Add to it the fact they'll be putting it before a national TV audience, and it makes the gravity of my mistake all the more egregious."

"I don't see how," a woman said.

"If I hadn't released the statement, a conservative news organization like CNC would never have gotten their hands on it, or even known about it. The investigation itself wasn't going anywhere within the bureau because the boy's story was so farfetched. In fact, they were just about to suspend it when I got fired."

"Mr. Fishburn put his arm around Vivian. "I wouldn't count too much on CNC being able to sell the kid's story, despite its appeal to so-called fundamentalists. I think most Americans will see it for what it is— a contrived, romanticized attempt to breathe new life into an ancient religious myth."

A combination of cheers and applause followed Ms. Scofield back to her seat. In Wendell's head, the wheels were already turning. He wasn't just concerned about how the boy's TV appearance might impact the public's perception of Christmas. Rather, he feared it could lead to a complete reversal of those declining Christianity statistics Mr. Fishburn had detailed at their last meeting.

Wendell stopped listening to the remaining items of business, as though someone had plugged his ears. His mouth was like cotton, and his heart beat like a steam-driven locomotive. Normally one of the last to depart the meetings, Wendell couldn't wait to get home so he could get to work.

This was the opportunity he'd been waiting for.

CHAPTER 24

Two days after meeting with Ms. Greene, Logan was in a deep sleep when he felt his mother gently touch his shoulder.

"Wake up, sweetheart," she said, leaning over him. "It's time to get up."

He looked at the clock on his dresser — 8:10.

His mother put some socks and underwear into a dresser drawer. "Someone's really taking advantage of their being out of school. I don't think I ever remember you sleeping this late before."

Logan tried to get up but felt groggier than he had the previous few days. When he swung his legs over the side of the bed, the room began to spin. "Ooh, I feel dizzy."

His mother put her arm around him. "Don't try to stand up if your head's spinning. Do you want to lay back down for a minute?"

"No, it's slowing down now. I think I'm all right."

"Are you sure?"

"Yeah, I'll get dressed and be right out."

A few minutes later, Logan joined his parents at the breakfast table.

"How are you feeling now?" Mom said.

"Better, except for this headache. At least the room stopped spinning."

"Maybe we should take him to the doctor," Mom said.

Dad twisted his mouth. "For a headache and a little dizziness?"

"He's been complaining of grogginess for a few days. Now dizziness and a headache."

"Okay, but does he have a fever?"

Mom touched his forehead. "Doesn't feel like one."

"Any diarrhea, vomiting?"

"Nothing like that, Dad," Logan said.

His mother brought him two children's Tylenol tablets. "Here, these will help your headache." She sat at the table and turned to his stepdad. "I just want to make sure he's not coming down with something. His interview is in two days."

"Maybe you should contact Ms. Greene about canceling or postponing."

Logan looked up from his plate of waffles, close to tears. "No, Mom, please. Don't do that. I don't feel that bad, honest."

The family went back to eating their breakfast in silence before the sound of Mom's fork striking her plate drew everyone's attention. She glared at Dad. "You conniving—" She cursed at her husband. It was the first time Logan had ever heard his mother use profanity. "You increased his dosage, didn't you?"

"Karen, please. We agreed not to talk about this in front of him."

"Increased my dosage of what?" Logan said.

Mom stood and crossed her arms. "You planned this all along, didn't you?" She cursed again. "To prevent Logan from being interviewed. What did you do, go back to Dr. Flo and get her to increase the prescription, or did you just do that on your own?"

Logan's stomach fluttered. "Put more of what in? What're you all talking about?"

Dad sat in silence, his face red.

Mom faced Logan. "Because you were so fearful of taking your medicine, I agreed with your father to mix it in with your food. That was wrong, and I apologize for being deceitful with you."

Logan couldn't believe what he was hearing. His own parents drugging him? He didn't know who he was more angry with—his mother for going along, or his stepfather for plotting to keep him from doing the interview. At least now he had an explanation for why he'd been feeling so bad lately. He shoved his plate of waffles away.

"Dr. Simonetti said he needs to be medicated," Dad said

"Medicated," Mom said. "Not turned into a zombie."

"Obviously, the initial dose wasn't working. He'd been on it for three days and still he told the story in school that got him suspended. So I called Dr. Simonetti and she upped his prescription from two to four milligrams a day. I was just following her instructions."

"Oh, you were, were you? And you didn't feel any obligation to tell me about it? I'm his mother for goodness sake."

"Why would I? As his mother, you agreed to the initial course of treatment, remember?"

"I did. And I'm not ashamed to admit it may have been the biggest mistake of my life. All the drug has done is to make Logan feel out of sorts. It's done nothing to inhibit his belief in the delusion, which, to me, is evidence he doesn't have one."

"Now you're starting to sound like Agent Garraway."

"Funny you should mention his name. The other day you told him Logan had become a laughingstock. But the truth is, you're the one who's afraid of becoming the laughing stock."

"Karen, like it or not, I work for one of the most prestigious investment firms on Wall Street. And as a senior member of the firm, I have a duty to protect its reputation from being tarnished."

"And just how does doping our son into near catatonia help that?"

Dad pushed away from the table. "I don't have time for this, Karen. I have to get to work." He gathered his things and headed for the front door.

"That's it," Mom said. "As of now, he's off the medication."

Dad shook his head and stormed out of the condo for a second time in three days.

"From now on, I don't want you accepting so much as a glass of water from your father without my being there, do you understand?"

"Yes, Mom."

"And for heaven's sake, don't fall for him offering you any candy."

* * *

With just two days before the broadcast, Wendell couldn't believe his good fortune. Mr. Childress had assigned his crew to clean the group of studios that included Studio 6, the precise location of Laurin

Greene's scheduled interview with Logan Ailshie. While his co-workers cleaned in other parts of the studio, Wendell spent nearly an hour vacuuming the white curved couch placed on an elevated platform in the middle of the set. Such meticulous cleaning activities served a dual purpose, the second being to conduct a thorough examination of the couch to find the best place to secrete his pipe bomb.

Placing his device wouldn't be easy. The doors to each of the studios were kept locked when not being cleaned, Mr. Childress being in possession of the only key. Which meant that to plant the bomb, Wendell would have to do it while his fellow crew members were in the room. Even waiting until one of them went to use the restroom would be risky. Complicating matters, Wendell's examination of the couch showed no viable way to tuck the bomb beneath the cushions or between the backrest and seat foundation without being detected. No choice but to access the underside of the couch.

At two o'clock in the morning, the crew broke for dinner. His colleagues, Andre and Martha, sat together on the couch. Wendell retrieved his backpack, moved around to the back of the couch and sat at floor level behind it.

"What're you doing down there, boy?" Andre turned around and leaned against the backrest. "Why don't you come up here where it's comfortable?"

"No thanks. When I'm done eating, I'm going to stretch out for a few minutes, use my backpack as a pillow."

"Plenty of room for you on the couch," Martha said.

Wendell forced a smile. "Thanks anyway."

A door opened, followed by the sound of footsteps. "Where's Wendell," a voice that sounded like Mr. Childress's said.

Wendell jumped up from behind the couch. "Right here, Mr. Childress."

"I need you to hotfoot it over to Studio 4. Kevin Stuart's gone home sick and I need someone to fill in for him the rest of the night."

Wendell's heart sank. What was he going to do now? "Can I eat first?"

"No. Take your dinner with you and get over there right away."

"But what about Martha and Andre? I don't want to leave them to clean this place by themselves."

"Don't worry about us, kid, we'll make out," Andre said.

"Plus, there's much more to clean over in Studio 4." Mr. Childress clapped his hands in quick succession. "Come on, let's go."

Wendell picked up his backpack and followed his supervisor out the door. He only had one more night to plant his device, and he was sure his cleaning assignment for tomorrow didn't include a tour in Studio 6.

* * *

Seated in his living room, Marcus looked up from his reading surprised at where the night had gone. His watch read 10:33 p.m. If not for work in the morning, he'd have continued with his study of the book of Romans. And with the anticipation of Logan's interview tomorrow weighing on his psyche, he needed to get some sleep.

Three nights ago, he came home from work, ate left-over Kung Pao chicken, watched the news, and readied himself for bed. He sat on the comforter and picked up the picture of Carolyn from the night stand. "Have I told you lately how much I miss you?" Feeling his eyes moisten, he returned the photograph. He opened the night stand drawer, pulled out the Bible she'd given him for his birthday, and turned to the inscription.

Marcus,

You once asked me how I could believe in the existence of something for which there is no tangible proof. And while I was more than happy to try to explain the concept of faith to you, I realize now that was a mistake. To truly understand it, you must investigate it for yourself.

This book will not only teach you who God is, but will also help you to better understand me, to give answer to all those questions you've posed over the years. Why I love Christmas and Easter so much, why I enjoy going to church, and why prayer is so important to me.

But beware, my love. If you attempt to interpret the Bible using only that wonderfully gifted, analytical mind of yours, you will fail. You must open your heart and allow the Holy Spirit to reveal to you the truth of the Scriptures, for "they are spiritually discerned."

I invite you to begin your journey in the Gospel of Luke, which is one of the four books about Jesus's life, and the only one that describes His birth in any detail.

Happy birthday, Darling,
Love, Carolyn

This time, he couldn't bridle his emotion, wiping away tears on his pajama sleeve. He lay on the bed, propped himself up against the headboard with pillows and opened his Bible to the Gospel of Luke.

Marcus maintained his normal reading pace through chapter one. However, at the beginning of chapter two, something changed. Even though he recognized some of the passages from previous Christmas Eve services, he still got goosebumps reading about the birth of Christ and the angels' annunciation to the shepherds. Several times he'd stop in mid-sentence, then re-read from the beginning before moving on to the next passage. It read like a verbatim account of Logan's statement to the FBI. So captivated by the parallel, he re-read the entire chapter five times before moving on to finish the first book.

For the next two evenings, Marcus continued his study of the Gospels, reading through Matthew and Mark the first night and John the next. What captured his attention the most wasn't Jesus's ability to perform miracles, but rather His display of wisdom, humility, and gentleness right up to His death. Marcus finally understood the meaning of a phrase his wife had quoted years ago from one of the prophets, "he was like a gentle lamb led to the slaughter."

At the same time, he couldn't ignore the clues to his own investigation that were being revealed during his research. Each healing miracle performed by Jesus provided yet another piece of circumstantial evidence to support Logan's own claim of supernatural healing.

After reading John, Marcus had fully intended to go to bed, but made the mistake of turning the page to see what came next. When he read about the coming of the Holy Spirit in the book of Acts, he vowed to stop at the end of the first chapter. Two and a half hours later, he completed the entire book before falling asleep at 1:15 in the morning.

Now, lying in bed reflecting on his walk along the Roman road to Salvation, he considered his first prayer since he was a child. After all this time, would it do any good? Would God even be listening? The thought of having his prayer rejected almost caused him to can the idea. But he remembered something from his study of the Gospels. Jesus's acceptance of the thief on the cross had proven it was never too late to come to God. He turned off the nightstand light, but kept his eyes open in the darkened room, a gesture to let the Lord know he was searching for Him.

"Lord God, I bet You never thought You'd be hearing from me. And to be honest, I never thought I'd be talking to You. Still, I thank You for Carolyn's reminder the other night that led me to finally open your Word. Lord, You've shown me so many things the past few nights. Some I don't understand. Things to challenge my beliefs, my view of the world. Fortunately, I found a quote that applies perfectly to me. It's from a father whose son Jesus healed and it says, 'Help my unbelief.' That is what I'm asking you tonight, Father, to help my unbelief. I also pray you won't hold it against me that it took me so long to come to you. In Jesus's name. Amen."

Marcus couldn't explain it, but a warm feeling swept over him at the thought Carolyn had just smiled down at him. "Good night, Carolyn."

CHAPTER 25

Wendell checked his cell phone for text messages for the third time in the last twenty minutes.

Sure enough, Mr. Childress had his crew working in Studio 2, one of the CNC Business programming studios located on the complete opposite side of the building from Studio 6. This made it near impossible for Wendell to slip over there unnoticed. Still, he had a plan, which included bribing a co-worker named Vince to switch work assignments with him without their boss's knowledge.

Wendell offered Vince twenty dollars, but he balked. "If we get caught, twenty dollars isn't going to go very far until I get my first unemployment check." Eventually, he settled for fifty dollars. Questioned why he wanted to switch so badly, Wendell told him Sylvia Alverez, a young Hispanic girl working on the other crew, had the hots for him.

Their plan relied on Mr. Childress keeping to his usual check-in schedule. This included oversight visits to each of the studios twice during the night, once during the first half and another during the second. That night, Wendell received a text from Vince that their boss had just left his second stop at Studio 6. Childress wouldn't return for two to four hours.

Wendell grabbed his backpack and hurried to Studio 6, high-fiving Vince as they passed each other in the hallway. When he got there, he secured one of the vacuum cleaners and headed to the area behind the curved couch. After a quick scan to locate the other custodians, he examined the underside of the couch. He pulled a utility knife from his backpack and carefully cut away a small area of the dustcover fabric.

Reaching into his backpack, he seized the pipe bomb. But before he pulled it out, Sylvia Alverez scurried across the floor of the studio and jumped, knees first, onto the couch. Wendell looked up to find her head and shoulders hanging over the backrest staring down at him.

"Hola, Wendell," she said, her English slurred by a thick Spanish accent. "You didn't even say hello to me when you came in. Are you upset with me? Or perhaps just ignoring me?"

Wendell dropped the pipe, wincing at the sound of it striking the floor through the bottom of the bag. "Now how could I ever be upset with you, senorita? And to ignore you would make me a fool."

Sylvia giggled. "Oh, Wendell. I don't yet understand all your words. But they sound so nice."

"Thank you." Wendell didn't want to offend her, or worse, make her suspicious, but he had to get rid of her. *Flattery. That should do it.* "Tell me something, are all the women from El Salvador as pretty as you?"

She giggled again, then cocked her head. "No . . . they're not." They both laughed together. "Will we be eating together?" she said.

"If I can. I may have to return to work in the other studio. But I hope to."

"Your loss if you don't." Sylvia turned her nose up, hopped off the couch, and left for another area of the studio.

Wendell returned his focus beneath the couch. He grabbed the pipe bomb and secured it between the springs and the frame of the couch's suspension. Flipping on the vacuum cleaner, he used a hand-held staple gun to re-attach the dustcover.

When he finished, he texted Vince advising him he was on his way. He picked up his backpack and headed out the studio door, only to run into Mr. Childress on the way out. "What're you doing over here?" the supervisor said.

Wendell felt his heartbeat racing. "Uh . . . uh, uh, I asked Vince to switch with me for a little while so I could talk to Sylvia."

"Oh, you did, did you?"

"While we were working, of course."

Childress's nostrils flared. "This isn't a single's bar, Schlump, or a dating service. And custodians don't switch their own work assignments. Now get your butt back over to Studio 2, and if I catch you over here again, you'll find yourself looking for another job. Is that clear?"

"Yes, Mr. Childress. Please accept my apologies. I appreciate this job." Wendell bowed slightly before leaving. However, once out of sight, he skipped down the hallway. Not only had he not gotten fired, which he fully expected, but this time he'd managed to get his device planted. And tomorrow night, at precisely 9:20 p.m. eastern standard time, this pimply-faced nerd from the Bronx would find himself catapulted into the annals of history.

9:20 p.m. tomorrow . . . Boom!

Though exhausted, Wendell was too excited to sleep when he got home the next morning. Instead, he replayed the many possible scenarios that might result from his act of defiance against Christian authority. On the one hand, a part of him felt guilty that a young boy and possibly others would die in the explosion. But that guilt was overshadowed by what he considered to be the larger picture—the significance of the statement, which would have historical impact. He'd already set his DVR to record Logan's interview so that he'd have a permanent record of his accomplishment. One he could watch over and over.

Wendell removed the second of his two pipe bombs from his backpack, an extra in case there was a problem planting the first. He had to disarm the timing mechanism, which had been set for the same time as the other. First, he tried twisting off one of the two endcaps, but it was locked tight, then the other, but it, too, wouldn't budge. Using a butter knife, he tapped along the edge of both endcaps but still couldn't get them to move.

Wendell's head pounded with the first signs of a building headache. He slammed his fist on the table and cursed.

Despite the danger, he banged one end of the pipe against the top of the table before making another attempt to twist off one of the endcaps. This time the cap broke free and twisted easily in his hand but stuck again when it reached the end of the thread line. Using all his strength, he gave the cap a final grunting twist.

The pipe bomb exploded.

Wendell's last sight was of a bright flash and his left hand disappearing from his forearm, his last feeling, shrapnel ripping through his skull and upper torso.

* * *

Late in the afternoon, Agent Garraway pulled up next to a slew of police vehicles in front of a small two-story building on 10th Avenue in Chelsea. He'd received a call from Detective Sean Mahoney advising him they'd found information in Schlump's apartment possibly related to his missing person investigation. Marcus had just exited his car when Todd and Janice showed up. Together, the trio entered the building and ascended the stairs to Mr. Schlump's apartment on the second floor. As expected, the place was in chaos, with pieces of wood, metal, human tissue, and blood scattered everywhere. Mr. Schlump's body had already been removed by the Medical Examiner's Office.

Detective Mahoney, wearing latex gloves, approached them as they entered the room. "Some mess, huh?"

"Yeah," Marcus said. "Who was this guy before he turned himself into confetti?"

The detective flipped open his notebook. "Wendell Schlump, white male, twenty-three, lived here for the past three years. Neighbors say he kept to himself. Works as a custodian on the night shift for Allied Cleaning Services in Manhattan."

"You said you found something that might be related to our case?"

Detective Mahoney gestured to another part of the

room. "Over here." He led them to a blood-splattered calendar hanging on the wall. In the block for today's date were the hand printed words "Logan Ailshie interview."

"Anything else?" Marcus said.

"A couple of newspapers on his bed containing articles about the leaked statement. We also found some clippings on the floor regarding an explosion that took place outside a local church on New Year's. Then there's all this." The detective swept his arm around the room, gesturing to the posters adorning the walls. "I don't see this dude spending a lot of time in church."

"Not without a gun to his head," Janice said.

"There's more." Detective Mahoney moved to the suspect's bed, picking up a mid-sized "Keep Christ OUT OF Christmas" sticker sign and some anti-Christian pamphlets. "We found these in one of the drawers of his dresser."

Janice examined the items, then showed the sign to Marcus while tapping with her thumb the name and contact info for "Manhattan Atheists" printed near the bottom.

Marcus raised an eyebrow of recognition but resisted the urge to react further lest he invite questions from the on-scene NYPD detectives. Vivian Scofield's association with the group was an internal matter. No need to air the bureau's dirty laundry, even in front of another law enforcement agency.

Detective Mahoney kneeled in front of the bookcase, though damaged, remained standing. He picked up three volumes lying on the floor. "Look at this. Mein Kampf, biographies of Kaczynski, the Tsarnaev brothers." He dropped the books, then slid his fingers along one of the shelves. "Looks like he's got every Atheist philosopher who ever published so much as a grocery list."

"What about bomb-making materials?" Marcus said.

Detective Mahoney flipped the page in his notebook. "Some black powder, wire, batteries, and, of course, tools."

"No other sections of pipe or endcaps?"

"None."

"This Schlump have a sheet?"

"One arrest for assault. But get this, it was for initiating a fight with one of the actors at a live Nativity Scene on Christmas Eve."

"Man, this guy really had it in for Christians, didn't he?" Todd said and turned to address Marcus. "Think he had something planned for Logan?"

Marcus put a hand to his chin. "I don't know. The kid's about to become a celebrity." He pointed to one of the posters. "And for all the wrong reasons, according to this guy's philosophy. Maybe he figured to stop him."

"But how?" Todd said. "The broadcast is tonight. What was he going to do, place the bomb outside his apartment door and ring the doorbell? Attach it to the underside of his parents' car in broad daylight?"

"Now you know why I called you," Detective Mahoney said. "I know it doesn't really shed any new light on your missing person case. But we figured you'd want to know about someone possibly planning an assassination of your victim. Lucky for him, ol' Wendell here blew himself up first. Case closed."

Lucky all right. Call it his suspicious nature, or maybe it was his cop instincts, but something wasn't setting right with Marcus. Schlump blowing himself up just hours before the broadcast seemed too darn convenient. Marcus scanned the room again, pausing to view the actions of the two NYPD evidence technicians working on opposite sides of the apartment. "How much longer do you figure to be?"

"Probably a couple of more hours yet. Don't worry, we'll let you know if we find anything else."

"Okay, thanks. Appreciate the call."

"Don't mention it."

Two minutes later, Todd and Janice stood with their supervisor outside of his black Chevy Suburban SUV. "I want you two to go down to this Allied Cleaning Services," Marcus said. "Find out who this Schlump's supervisor is. Interview him and anyone else Schlump worked with. Find out everything you can about him, particularly if anyone heard him make any threats against the Ailshie boy."

Todd cleared his throat. "Begging your pardon, boss, but isn't this the PD's case? Aren't we going to be stepping on their toes by conducting follow-up interviews of their witnesses?"

"You heard what Mahoney said. They've all but closed the case as an accidental death. Which means they won't get around to conducting any follow-up interviews for a couple of days. I want to know the answers to those questions *before* the broadcast tonight."

"Got it."

"What about Vivian Scofield?" Janice said.

"I'll talk to her myself."

"I wouldn't count on her being too cooperative."

"I'm hoping she'll have some sympathy when she finds out it's one of her fellow Manhattan Atheists who got zapped."

CHAPTER 26

At 8:58 p.m., Marcus crossed the Manhattan Bridge into lower Manhattan on his way back from Vivian Scofield's home in Crown Heights. To his surprise, she had been extremely cooperative, if not overly helpful. Yes, she knew Wendell Schlump from their monthly organizational meetings, but no, she knew nothing of any threat made by him against Logan Ailshie. She described Wendell as an ardent and vocal supporter of the atheist cause, almost to the point of being a fanatic. However, her personal opinion was that he was more bark than bite.

Marcus answered an incoming cell phone call from Todd. "Tell me something good, Todd."

"You're going to want to kiss me. Wendell Schlump worked as a custodian cleaning the CNC Studios. And get this — last night he paid one of his co-workers to switch assignments with him so he could work in the studio where they're interviewing the Ailshie kid tonight."

"Nice work, Todd. Listen, I'm about ten minutes from there. Contact NYPD and have them dispatch a bomb disposal unit to the studio right away. Then you and Janice meet me there as quick as you can."

"What on earth for? Schlump's dead. He went up

185

in smoke, and his bomb with him."

"No. You had it right this afternoon when you said Schlump wouldn't have had an opportunity to plant his bomb before tonight's broadcast. That's because he'd already planted it. The bomb that blew him up this morning was his backup, a secondary device in case something went wrong with the first. He probably detonated it when he tried to defuse it."

Marcus disconnected the call, hit the emergency lights in the Suburban, and mashed the accelerator to get every extra horse he could out of the engine. How much time did he have? When would Wendell have set his device to go off? Surely not at nine o'clock on the dot. Even with a short introductory monologue by the host, and maybe a commercial thrown in, Logan might not yet be on stage. Surely he wouldn't have set it that early. And by nine-thirty, the boy would have told half his story, perhaps more. The bomber wouldn't have wanted to wait that late—9:15. That was the sweet spot.

Marcus flew past the three Canal Street subway stations near the Broadway and Lafayette intersections before slowing to turn right onto 6th Avenue, heading north. His dashboard clock read 9:03. He accelerated to 65 miles per hour, weaving in and out of traffic and avoiding obstacles with judicious use of the gas pedal, brakes, and steering wheel.

A minute later, he crossed over W 14th Street, his speedometer reading 69 miles per hour as he blew through a red light at the intersection, barely missing a taxicab.

At W 39th Street, a green Honda Accord pulled in front of him, prompting a jerk of the steering wheel hard to avoid a collision. He slammed on the brakes, but it was too late. Marcus struck the curb on the left side of the street, blowing out the left front tire and lifting the SUV up onto its two right wheels. It nearly flipped before righting itself and sliding some ninety feet along the sidewalk. Just before the SUV came to rest, a young man in a red skull cap dove out of the way.

Marcus got out and ran to help the man, who had already started to get up on his own. Seeing the man wasn't seriously injured, Marcus apologized and hurried back to his vehicle.

The clock read 9:14.

He floored the SUV and traveled less than a block when the blown tire tore away from the rim, shooting sparks out the left side of the undercarriage. Marcus fought to steer in a straight line. But he refused to let up on the accelerator, reaching a speed of 44 miles per hour on the disintegrating rim.

Crossing W 47th Street, he eased off the gas and pumped the brakes. The SUV tried to veer right, but Marcus held a tight rein on the steering wheel. The vehicle came to rest 20 yards shy of the 6th Avenue entrance to CNC headquarters. Marcus hurried from the vehicle and sprinted toward the CNC Building.

The time was 9:17.

No people or smoke streamed from the building.

At most, he had mere minutes, perhaps seconds until detonation.

Sirens approached in the distance, but he raced into the building. The guard at the front desk pointed him to the location of the studio where the broadcast was being aired — down the hallway and to the right.

Seconds later, the agent burst through the studio door but was immediately confronted by a cameraman and a male producer. Marcus flashed his credentials and uttered one word, "Bomb." The three men moved quickly toward the set where Ms. Greene and Logan chatted on the couch.

When Logan saw Marcus, a big smile graced his lips. "Agent Garraway. What are you—"

Marcus lifted the boy into his arms while the other two men ushered Laurin off the opposite side of the stage. Marcus took one step with Logan before they were thrown to the ground by an explosion behind them.

He and Logan cried out while being tossed onto the floor.

Pain seared Marcus's right scapula, left buttocks, and left calf from flying shrapnel.

A female producer behind the cameras screamed. "Go to commercial. Go to commercial!"

Marcus had tried to shield Logan with his body, but the boy's whimpering told him he hadn't been entirely successful. "Are you hit?" he said.

Logan rolled onto his back, holding his hand just above the waist. Blood seeped between his fingers onto a light blue polo shirt. "Yeah, but I don't think it's that bad."

"Paramedic!" Marcus shouted. "Do you guys have a paramedic or EMT on staff?"

"No," another cameraman said. "But we'll get one here right away. I'll get our first aid kit."

Mrs. Thomas charged through the hallway door screaming her son's name. She knelt beside him. "Are you all right?"

"It's okay, Mom."

"But you're bleeding. Let me see."

She tried to lift his shirt, but Marcus restrained

her. "It's best to let him keep pressure on it for now," he said. "Someone's bringing a first aid kit."

Laurin and the other two studio employees, none of whom was injured, returned to where Marcus and Logan lay on the floor. Laurin took the first aid kit from the returning cameraman and knelt to treat Logan and Marcus's injuries.

"Wait a minute." Temporarily distracted by the explosion, Marcus had forgotten his first duty — the protection of lives. "Not here."

"But we need to stop the bleeding," Laurin said.

"I know." Marcus winced while forcing himself from the floor. "Listen, everyone. The bomb squad is on the way. But we need to clear this area immediately in case there's a secondary device planted."

The cameraman picked up Logan, and Laurin and another man helped Marcus to his feet. Everyone was evacuated from the studio, and the injured taken to the main lobby for first aid and to await arrival of the ambulance.

CHAPTER 27

Several hours later, Logan woke up groggy in a hospital bed with his parents standing over him. "Wha . . . what happened?" he whispered.

His mother stroked his forehead. "It's all over now. You had to have an operation. The doctors removed a piece of shrapnel that was lodged near one of your kidneys."

Logan blinked rapidly. "Am I going to be all right?"

"Of course you are. The shrapnel missed all of the major organs. If there's no infection, the doctor said you might be able to go home tomorrow. In a couple of weeks, you'll be good as new."

He sighed before realizing he'd forgotten something. He tried to raise his head off the pillow, but dizziness forced him back down. "What happened to Agent Garraway?"

"Why don't you ask him yourself. He's in the bed right next to you."

Agent Garraway was propped up in his bed. "About time you woke up. I thought I was going to have to ask the nurse to throw some water on your head."

"Ah, come on," Logan studied the agent's

bandaged left leg. "How are you feeling?"

"Put it this way. I won't be pitching for the Mets or dancing with the stars anytime soon. Other than that, I'm pretty good."

The door opened and a middle-aged man wearing a white coat entered and walked past Agent Garraway's bed. "Good morning, everyone."

"Logan," Mom said, "this is Dr. O'Keefe. He's the one who operated on you."

"Pleased to meet you," Logan said. "My mom said you might let me go home tomorrow?"

"A distinct possibility, provided we can get some food into you." Dr. O'Keefe pulled back the covers to examine the wound and the surgical incision on the boy's side. "Looks good. This glue should peel off on its own in about a week. Until then, he can shower, but I wouldn't immerse him in a bathtub."

"We understand," Mom said.

Dr. O'Keefe covered his mouth and dropped his chin, as if deep in thought.

"Doctor," Mom said. "Is there something else?"

He continued to stare at the floor for a moment, then his head snapped up. "Actually, there was something else I needed to discuss with you." He glanced at Agent Garraway. "We can step out in the hallway if you prefer privacy."

"Agent Garraway just saved our son's life. I figure that entitles him to hear anything you have to say."

"Something strange showed up on your son's x-ray when we were prepping him for surgery."

"Something strange," Dad said. "You mean something other than the shrapnel?"

"Yes. And to be sure, we followed up the x-ray with an ultrasound of Logan's abdomen."

Logan's mother covered her mouth with both hands. "Oh, no! You found a tumor."

"No, no, Mrs. Thomas, nothing like that," the doctor said. "Your son was brought to this hospital two years ago for an emergency appendectomy, is that correct?"

"Yes," she said.

"And the surgeon performed the procedure laparoscopically?"

"Yes, why?"

"Mr. and Mrs. Thomas. As a doctor, this is very difficult for me to explain. As a matter of fact, there isn't a medical explanation for it."

"Doctor," Dad said, "what is it?"

"There's no evidence your son ever had his appendix removed. There are no scars on his belly from the laparoscopic procedure, and—"

"And what, doctor?" Dad said.

"The ultrasound shows the presence of a normal, healthy appendix."

Wow! Logan struggled to concentrate through the slowly fading effects of the anesthesia. Jesus must have given him his appendix back, too.

Logan's parents stared wide-eyed at each other. "How can that be?"

"Like I said, I can't explain it. Your son had three holes cut into his abdomen and now they're gone. Even completely healed surgical incisions leave a scar."

His mother glanced at Dad, who nodded. "To be honest, doctor," she said. "We knew about the scars. Logan showed them to us a week ago. He thinks Jesus healed them when he traveled back in time."

Logan raised his head again. "But He did heal them, Mom."

"Are you familiar at all with our son's ordeal?" Mom stared as the doctor.

"I've seen the story in the papers."

Dad crossed his arms and leaned forward. "But an appendix can't just grow back, can it?"

Physiologically, it's impossible. Unlike tonsils, which can sometimes regenerate, once an appendix is gone, it's gone for good."

Mom touched her heart. "Oh, my goodness."

"You're saying it's a miracle?" Dad said.

"I'm saying, medical science doesn't have an explanation for it. Whether or not you consider that a miracle, I guess, depends on your point of view."

Dad frowned. He and Mom glanced over to the other bed.

"Don't look at me," Agent Garraway said. "I already told you, I believe in miracles. This only reinforces it."

Dr. O'Keefe entered some information on the screen of his iPad. "Miracle or not, I have a duty to notify you of any changes related to your son's health." He looked at the clock on the wall — 3:35 a.m. "There's still several more hours before daylight. These two should get some rest." He faced Logan's parents. "I'd advise you to do the same, that is if you don't mind stretching out on one of the couches in the waiting room down the hall."

"We're all right, doctor," Logan's mother said. "My husband has to go home and get ready for work. I'm going to stay right here and sleep in this chair." She sat in a chair next to a window across from Logan's bed.

After Dad said good-bye, he followed Dr. O'Keefe out of the room.

"Agent Garraway," a voice whispered.

Marcus thought he was dreaming that a small boy had called his name. The call repeated and his eyes fluttered open. Logan stood next to him in the shadowed room, a curtain drawn between their two beds.

"Agent Garraway."

The clock on the wall read five minutes after five. "Are you okay? What are you doing out of bed?"

"I had to use the bathroom. Can I talk to you?"

"Sure. Where's your mom?"

The boy motioned behind him. "Asleep in the chair."

Marcus scooted over on the bed. Every move hurt. "Sit down."

"Thanks. I wanted to thank you for . . ." Logan appeared deep in thought. "For—"

"Saving your life?"

A sheepish smile crossed the boy's mouth. "Yeah, well . . . that, too, but what I really wanted to thank you for is believing me."

Marcus's head jerked back slightly. "It wasn't hard. I told your dad last week that the evidence speaks for itself. And after hearing about your appendix, it just spoke a whole lot louder."

"You're the only one who does—outside of my mother and Ms. Greene, that is. My stepfather doesn't."

"Your stepfather isn't a religious man?"

"Just the opposite."

"Well, I wouldn't be too discouraged. I've come to learn each man must find his own way to God. Fact is, in some ways I was much like your stepfather—little, if any, faith. Thankfully, this case has given me a new perspective. How does he treat you otherwise?"

"In the six years I've known him, he's given me everything I wanted . . . except his time. Simeon spent more time with me in the week I was with him than my stepfather ever has."

"That has to be tough."

Logan dropped his eyes. "It has. When I was younger, I once asked my mother why my last name was different from theirs. I thought it was strange because I knew a couple of kids at school who'd been adopted. She said for the first few years after they were married, she always hoped he'd come to her with an offer to do the same, but he never did. When she finally got up the nerve to ask him about it, he always seemed to have an excuse for postponing the discussion. Eventually, she gave up.

Marcus patted Logan's leg. "I'm sorry."

"So, how do I go about getting my story out there now?"

"I'm not following you."

"No one's going to want to interview me after the bombing."

Marcus snorted. "Are you kidding me? If I know Laurin, she'll put the two of you in bomb disposal outfits and find a way to simulcast it worldwide."

"Do you really think so?"

"Two and a half million people just saw some nut try to silence you with a bomb on national TV. My feeling is you're going to have twice as many wanting to hear your message. Christian or not, Americans don't like people infringing on their freedom of speech. They'll tune in all right, for no other reason than their resentment that someone tried to stop you from delivering it."

"I hope so."

"Hey, I just remembered. I've got something of yours I've been meaning to give back to you. Can bring me my pants from the closet?"

Logan did as he was asked.

Marcus reached into his pants pocket and pulled out the copper coin the boy had given him. "By the way, do you know the story behind this coin?"

The boy's eyes widened. "There's a story that goes with it?"

"You bet. The coin is called a mite. Back in Jesus's time, a mite was one of the least valuable coins around. Kind of like a penny is today. One day, Jesus sat watching all these rich people putting a lot of money into the treasury. And the widow had only her two pennies to put in. But because those two pennies amounted to all the money she had, Jesus said she put in more than all those who were rich."

"So, you're saying it isn't really worth anything?"

He chuckled. "On the contrary. It may very well be the most valuable coin on earth."

Logan's face brightened. "Really? How?"

"Intrinsically, it might not be worth much more than the few cents worth of copper used to make it, but the fact it was given to you by Joseph makes it priceless."

"Cool."

"If I were you, though, I'd have my parents put it in a safe or a safe deposit box." Marcus glanced at the clock again. "It'll be light in a couple of hours. Why don't you get back to bed and catch a few winks?"

Logan started back to his side of the room but stopped and turned. "Agent Garraway, if you could do something to ensure your own happiness, but knew it would hurt someone close to you if you did, would you still do it?"

Marcus rubbed his chin. *Where's this coming from?* "I guess it would all depend on the circumstances. Is the happiness short- or long-term? Is the hurt temporary or permanent, minor or crushing? Ultimately, I'd say you'd have to follow your own heart."

"Thanks." Logan gripped the coin before returning to bed.

What a strange question, especially coming from a nine-year-old. What did Logan have on his mind?

CHAPTER 28

A week later, Marcus stopped by the Thomas's apartment on his way to work. He wanted to see how Logan was doing and to congratulate him on the success of his interview with Laurin Greene, which aired the previous evening. News reports on the radio said the special had garnered 25.4 million viewers, a record for a non-celebrity interview. Among those viewers was one Marcus Peter Garraway.

Following the show's intro, Laurin appeared on set in the foreground, seated on a stool in front of a large backdrop in the shape of an open book. The right-side page contained the name of the producer with the formatted story text written below it. On the left, a side view picture of Logan holding a model car filled two thirds of the frame. Above him, in a large holiday style font, appeared the title of the segment: "The Boy Who Cried Christmas."

"Good evening," Laurin said. "Tonight, we present the remarkable journey of Logan Ailshie, the nine-year-old boy who traveled from his New York City apartment, back in time, to the holy city of Bethlehem. There, he became an eyewitness to the most historic event in human history.

"As many of you know, this isn't our first attempt

to present Logan's story, which a week ago ended like this."

The producers switched to a replay of the explosion. When they switched back, Laurin and Logan were seated next to each other on a reproduction of the couch that'd been destroyed. "Despite sustaining a serious injury in the explosion, Logan has bravely and selflessly agreed to continue with the interview," she said.

"Logan's odyssey back in time lasted nine days. And when he came home," Laurin paused, leaning forward into the camera, "no one would believe him. Not even his parents. Because he was a child, people assumed he was either lying or dreaming or acting out a child's fantasy. Like other boys his age, Logan had made up stories. And so it became easy to portray him as just another congenital storyteller, a boy who cried wolf.

"But as you watch this story tonight, try to keep in mind this one salient point from Aesop's famous fable, a point perhaps overshadowed by the lesson of the parable itself.

"The last time the boy tried to warn the villagers about the wolf, he was telling the truth. And that is why we've chosen to title this story 'The Boy Who Cried Christmas.'"

Beginning with his contact with the homeless man outside the Chick-Fil-A, she walked Logan through the steps of his adventure.

Logan displayed both a calm and an exuberance when recounting the story and answering questions. During the interview, the producers spliced in video-taped file coverage from the site of his disappearance at the Thomas's East 63rd Street condo. Likewise, the director cut away to stock photos of ancient Bethlehem, flocks of sheep, Mary and Joseph, and the baby Jesus at corresponding points in Logan's story.

As only a child can do honestly, Logan displayed a full range of emotions throughout the interview. His eyes sparkled with wonder when he talked about meeting the baby Jesus, the legion of angels, and Mary and Joseph. Fear etched his face when discussing the wolf attack and being condemned to death by Herod. His voice seemed strongest, and his demeanor the most earnest, when speaking about his friendship with Simeon and the other shepherds.

After the last commercial break, Laurin was again shown seated on her stool in front of the opening backdrop. "Thank you for joining us this evening to share in Logan's journey. Whether you're a believer or not, his story provides a message of hope for a world that desperately needs it. Good night."

Marcus stood directly in front of the Thomases's door and rang the doorbell, anticipating a warmer reception than he'd received during his last visit. Indeed, Mrs. Thomas greeted him with a smile and invited him in.

Marcus scanned the apartment. "Where's the celebrity?"

"In his room." Mrs. Thomas called for Logan then offered Marcus a cup of coffee. When her son hadn't come out by the time she brought it, she went to his door and knocked. "Logan, did you hear me. Agent Garraway's here to see you."

Silence.

Mrs. Thomas entered the boy's room. After fifteen seconds, she screamed. "Brad! Agent Garraway!"

Both men hurried into the room. The first thing

Marcus noticed coming through the door was a drop in the temperature, followed by the boy's absence, then an open window on the far wall.

"Oh, no," Mr. Thomas said. "Not again." He flung open Logan's closet door.

"I already checked there." Mrs. Thomas put her face into her hands and cried.

Brad knelt on the floor to check under the bed, but quickly rose shaking his head. He and Marcus left the room to conduct a thorough search of the apartment.

When they returned, something appeared to draw Mrs. Thomas's attention to Logan's dresser. She picked up her son's iPhone and held it out in front of her. "Look. Something must have really happened to him. He'd never leave this behind."

Marcus paused to consider the revelation. Is this what Logan meant the other night when he asked his cryptic question? But dare he tell the Thomases his supposition concerning the boy's whereabouts? While it was almost certain to be discounted by Mr. Thomas, he had to for Mrs. Thomas's sake. "I don't think so."

"What do you mean you don't think so," Brad said. "Do you know something we don't?

Marcus notified the NYPD to respond to the Thomas residence for another missing person complaint. "The police are on the way. And when they get here they'll conduct another complete investigation. But in all honesty — "

Mrs. Thomas clutched her arms to her chest. "You know where he is, don't you?"

"I think so."

"Where! Please tell us where."

Marcus gestured to the phone in Mrs. Thomas's

hand. "Someplace where he won't need his phone." He offered his theory that Logan had been taken back in time again by his enigmatic benefactor, Robert, offering as proof the similar circumstances of his first disappearance. What he didn't tell them was his belief their son wouldn't be coming back this time.

True to form, Mr. Thomas once again brushed it off as nonsense.

The first patrol officers and investigators arrived at the condo fifteen minutes later, followed closely by Detective Mahoney, who supervised the processing of Logan's room for a record third time. Marcus, although fairly certain of the boy's whereabouts, concurred with Mahoney that a new lookout for Logan should be posted. Since the previous BOLO for Robert Templeton was still active, they agreed not to make any changes pending examination of any evidence found in the boy's bedroom.

On his way out of the apartment, Marcus paused at the door to again admire the charm and opulence of the Thomas's apartment, still beautifully decorated for Christmas. Logan had everything a boy could want. Except a father who loved him. Things must have been pretty bad for him to want to leave his mother in the hope of finding someone to fill that void.

CHAPTER 29

Marcus reached his apartment later that evening but hesitated when opening the door because he noticed light bathing the foyer wall inside. A light he hadn't left on. He drew and raised his service weapon, slowly opening the door with his other arm. He crept down the short hallway, past the kitchen on the left and into the living room where he found a man in a green army jacket seated on his couch.

"You're Robert Templeton." Marcus lowered the pistol.

Templeton nodded. "I see you were successful in identifying me since our last meeting. My compliments to you and your team on your investigative skills."

Marcus raised a single eyebrow. "You know you're a wanted man, don't you?"

"Are you planning to arrest me?"

Marcus holstered his weapon. "And have to explain to the world the arrest of a man who's been dead for seventy-six years? I don't think so. Not to mention, it goes against my grain to arrest American war heroes."

Templeton chuckled. "I'm no hero. I was just a young man looking to serve his country after the Japanese attack on Pearl Harbor. I went into the recruiting office the very next day, December 8th, but ended up being transferred to the European theater.

"What about your actions at Normandy? You don't consider that heroic?"

"Not really. The morning of June 6th was the most exciting day of my life. All the way across the English Channel I had butterflies in my gut. I couldn't wait to get to the fighting. My enthusiasm changed once we hit the beach."

"Pretty scary, huh?"

"Words can't describe it. Seeing all those men being blown to bits, decapitations, limbs blown off, entrails spread all over the beach. Ghastly. Robert cringed, and his voice cracked when he spoke. "On the day I was killed, I was like a little kid, crying my eyes out while crouched behind an iron hedgehog. Just before leaving my position, I remember thinking it would be better to get struck by a bullet and killed instantly than to continue to cower on the beach. Anyway, I threw caution to the wind and charged one of the two enemy emplacements that was doing the most damage to my platoon. It was a miracle I made it to the bunker without being struck by one of those bullets whizzing by my head."

"Still, the army credited you with saving, what was it, thirty lives? Your actions meant a lot."

"Thank you for the recognition, but I did what I was trained to do."

Marcus went into the kitchen, pulled out an open bottle of Jack Daniels from the cabinet, and raised it in front of him. "Drink?"

"No, thank you."

"I guess angels don't drink, do they?" He poured himself a drink and sat in a chair next to Private

Templeton. "So, what happened to Logan? You send him back to Bethlehem?"

"It's where he wanted to go."

"I thought you told him God wanted him to spread the message of Christmas."

"And he did . . . with your help."

"My help. What did I do?"

"If you remember, it was you who suggested the Thomases contact Ms. Greene about doing an interview with Logan."

"Oh, that wasn't—"

"There's more. Not only did you go on to save his life, but by doing so in such dramatic fashion on national television, you ensured a ten-fold increase in the reach of his message. Exactly the outcome you predicted to Logan in the hospital."

"I know, but what's going to happen now that he's gone?"

"It'll still have legs. Someone will write a book, which will be turned into a movie, which will end up being played every year during the holidays. Add to it the circumstances of Logan's mysterious disappearance, and his story will draw Amelia Earhart-like interest for decades. Besides, this was as much about you as it was about Logan."

Marcus stiffened.

"Sure, God was concerned the true message of Christmas was being stifled, although that's been going on in this country for well over a hundred years. But His more immediate concern was for you, Marcus."

"Me? Why me?"

"Because of your misguided hatred for it based on the death of your wife."

"Guess He knows about that, too, huh?"

"Of course. He also knows your thoughts of suicide. But in this case, He received a special request to intercede on your behalf."

"A request? From who?"

"Your wife Carolyn."

Marcus's drink slipped from his hand and bounced off his thigh. He caught the glass before it hit the floor, spilling Jack on his pants, the chair, and the carpet. "Excuse me." He retrieved a hand towel and sopped up the spill, then refilled his glass and returned to his seat. "Now what's this about a request from Carolyn?"

"She couldn't bear to see you go through the rest of your life on earth hating Christmas. She thought if you could be made to understand its true meaning, and why it was so important to her, you wouldn't hate it any longer. So, she asked the Lord for help. This was His answer."

An audience with Jesus. Wow! He must have put some pretty heavy stock in her to grant her request. "Are you saying this whole thing was planned out in advance?"

"Absolutely. Logan's going back in time. Your being assigned to supervise the investigation into his disappearance. It was all orchestrated by the Lord so you would come to believe Jesus is the Son of God. And in believing, you would be able to share in your wife's love of Christmas."

"So, that's what you meant when you told me in the cemetery I needed Logan's help?"

"Exactly. Your fates were intertwined. Separately, each of you was going through your own crisis of faith. Your investigation of his disappearance produced clues confirming to you the deity of Christ. You saved his life so he could deliver God's message." Robert offered a confident smile.

"Okay, so I believe in Jesus, and I understand the significance of His birthday. How do I get past the hurt of losing Carolyn on that day?"

Robert shook his head. "I'll admit it's hard to conflate two opposing emotions — overwhelming joy and gut-wrenching grief — on the same day. If it were up to me, no one would ever die at Christmas."

"Sure would make it easier for a lot of us to enjoy the holiday."

"Since you're reading your Bible, I'd like to point out several passages you might find encouraging. Quotes to remind you that death can be looked upon as a gift, rather than something to be feared. Take a look at Ecclesiastes 7:1, 2 Corinthians 5:8, and Philippians 1:21. Fact is, for those who die in Christ, like Carolyn, there is no death, only the transition to another life."

"Funny, she used to say the same thing."

"Keep reading your Bible and you'll find it out for yourself. Here are a few other things to help reduce the pain of losing her at Christmas. Don't make December 25th just about Jesus. Make it a celebration of your wife as well. After all, it may have been His first day on earth, but it was her first day in heaven. Also, why not try doing some of the things she used to love to do at Christmas, like decorating your apartment, putting up a tree, or — "

"If you say baking cookies, angel or not, I'm going to slug you."

Robert snickered. "No, I wasn't going to say that, but I was going to suggest you go back to church, at least on Christmas Eve, as a memorial to her."

"That I can handle."

"Do you donate to charity?"

"Not much since Carolyn died."

"Well, then, now's a good time to resume. Better yet, create your own foundation that accepts donations at Christmas and name it for your wife. Donate the money to whatever charity was her favorite."

"That would be Samaritan's Purse."

"All of these things should help to trigger fond memories of Carolyn. There'll still be times when you'll feel a bit melancholy. But once you begin to view Christmas as another opportunity to celebrate her life, rather than her death, you'll have little reason to hate it anymore."

"I'll try."

Robert stood. "I think you'll find it beats going into work on Christmas Day to avoid having to face it."

Marcus's attention was again drawn to the little red Christmas ball swinging from the man's buttonhole. Marcus paused to consider his next action, a handshake. Would his hand pass right through an incorporeal appendage? Or should he just forego the courtesy altogether? "I guess I should thank you for taking the time to stop by to tell me all this." When he extended his arm, he was surprised to feel the grip of what appeared to be a solid flesh and blood hand. After the handshake, Marcus headed for the door.

"Going somewhere?" Robert said.

"I was just going to escort you to the door."

"Thank you, but I'll go out the way I came in."

Marcus instinctively lifted an upraised palm toward the living room window. "Be my guest."

Robert walked to the window, opened it, and turned back to Marcus. "Farewell." Without moving a muscle, the soldier's body dissolved standing in front of the opening.

Marcus moved to close and lock the window. He chuckled inside. *Untidy creatures, these angels. You'd think they'd learn how to close a window.* If he had any lingering doubts about Robert's divine nature, they disappeared with him.

CHAPTER 30

December 24, One Year Later

Just before noon, Marcus parked his car on the path in front of his wife's headstone and reached to shut off the engine. A news item from the hourly recap broadcast on his car radio captured his attention. It said church attendance across the country during the past year had increased by an aggregate total of eleven percent across all denominations. Area pastors and priests were expecting to see a rise in Christmas Eve service attendance as well. To Marcus's surprise, the announcer gave credit to "Logan Ailshie, the missing ten-year-old whose holiday story of time travel and supernatural healing had captivated the nation."

The news report prompted Marcus to reflect on the impact Logan's story had on other aspects of everyday life, including the economy. Secular media had sought to blame him for an eight percent decrease in retail holiday sales so far this Christmas, citing his ability to refocus shoppers' priorities away from traditional purchases. Sales of automobiles, toys, even Coca-Cola were down, though strangely enough, purchases of Nativity scenes, angels, Bibles, and other religious items had skyrocketed.

From a personal standpoint, Marcus had grown exponentially during the past year, both as a Christian and a widower. He'd completed his second full reading of the New Testament and had learned enough to know what Carolyn had been trying to tell him over the years had been true. Now, he was focused on studying the Old Testament, having made it through to the book of Psalms. He'd gone back to church, not every Sunday, but enough so he could address most of his fellow parishioners by their first names. On April 16th, he was baptized on the anniversary of what would have been Carolyn's forty-second birthday.

For Christmas, he'd followed many of Robert's suggestions. In decorating his apartment, he put up a Nativity scene before anything else, followed by a tree, garland, knickknacks, and string lighting. He ordered a half-dozen eight by ten photographs taken of Carolyn in different Christmas settings from previous years to set amidst the decorations. His proudest achievement, however, was the creation of the Carolyn Garraway Survive the Holidays Foundation. The nonprofit's mission was to help families suffering from depression, alcoholism, or drug addiction brought on by the death of a loved one during the holidays. In this, their inaugural year, contributions had already exceeded thirty-one thousand dollars. The foundation's charter also called for the formation of a support group to provide in-person counseling and group therapy sessions run by a licensed grief counselor.

Marcus opened the car door and grasped the Christmas wreath lying on the passenger's seat before exiting. He made his way to Carolyn's grave, placing the wreath over the center arm of the headstone and down onto the two side arms. "Hello, Carolyn. Hard to believe it's been three years already. But then, the calendar doesn't lie, does it? And yes, I placed a Christmas wreath on your headstone. Surprised? Yeah, I am, too." He adjusted the wreath so the red bow at the bottom hung straight. "I hope you won't take my change in attitude as a concession I miss you any less. If anything, it makes me miss you more. I just don't blame God anymore for taking you. Anyway, I guess I have you and Robert to thank for that, huh?"

Marcus's attention was diverted by the sight of a few snowflakes falling around him. He pulled his overcoat collar up around his neck and lifted his head skyward, allowing the flakes to hit his face. He couldn't remember the last time it snowed in New York City for Christmas. "Oh, and the message you wrote in my Bible about faith . . . you were right. I really did have to investigate it for myself." Marcus checked his watch. "I have to go now. Your foundation is having a little Christmas Eve get together this afternoon and they've asked me to say a few words.

"If you see Robert up there, tell him he was right, too."

"Merry Christmas, Darling." He bent and kissed the headstone, then wiped the tear from his eye.

CHAPTER 31

Thirty-three years later

Forty-three-year-old Logan Ailshie stood on a hillside overlooking the largest flock of sheep in Bethlehem, thirteen thousand animals, of which eight thousand belonged to him. The remainder were owned by his close friends, Asher, with three thousand head, and Ephraim, with two thousand. Such was the legacy left to him by his father, Simeon, making Logan one of the richest and most highly-respected men in Israel.

But Logan's path to greatness wasn't lined with honeysuckle, beginning with the days immediately following his return to the time period. Just as Simeon had predicted, Herod's soldiers had returned to the shepherds' camp to conduct another search following their initial pursuit to Jericho and Kirjath Jearim. They returned again a few days later. And a few days after that. Fortunately, Eliab had kept Logan's disguise of a sheepskin, which he would quickly put on whenever they saw the soldiers approaching. Soon after, the shepherds moved their flocks back closer to Bethlehem and the soldiers stopped coming. Until about two years later.

Late one night, while the shepherds slept, Herod's

soldiers rode into their camp ordering everyone up. Only this time, Logan didn't have time to put on his disguise. He felt a weakness in his legs while the soldiers searched their belongings. Even though he'd grown some in the past two years, he was certain he'd be recognized. But he wasn't. After the solders completed their search, they rode away toward the town.

The next day, they received word the soldiers had murdered every male child two years of age and younger in Bethlehem and the surrounding villages.

Beyond fearing for his life, Logan's first six months back proved to be an adjustment. Though he genuinely loved being with Simeon and the other shepherds, he did miss his mother. He also missed watching television, playing video games, the iPhone he'd just received for Christmas, and Chick-Fil-A. Loss of these activities was offset by his training as a shepherd, a steadfast commitment to learn the Scriptures, and his deepening friendship with Ephraim, Asher, and Perez. After a while, he even stopped wondering about what he might be missing in the future.

A year following the murders in Bethlehem, Simeon held a celebration that Logan supposed was to mark the end of a successful harvest season. All of their friends and neighbors had been invited, a gathering of over fifty men and their families. Simeon stood before them to announce he'd taken steps to adopt Logan, granting him title to his name and all his property. A widower for the past thirty-eight years, Simeon had been married for only three years before his wife died of a fever, leaving him without an heir. Logan, after having one father abandon him and another deny him, finally felt like he belonged to someone. His proudest moment was the first time he addressed Simeon as "Father." It was a day he'd come to mark every year thereafter for the remainder of his life.

When Logan was twenty-nine, he, Simeon, and their friends attended the annual sheep-shearing festival held for the shepherds of Bethlehem and the surrounding region. A festival characterized by a celebratory atmosphere of feasting and drinking, it was often attended by entire families, including women and children. One of the attendees was a young girl named Naomi, considered by many to have been the most beautiful girl at the festival and the daughter of one of Simeon's oldest friends. Introduced to her at the celebration, Logan found himself attracted as much to her wisdom and gentleness as to her beauty.

A year later, the couple were married, and the year after, he and Naomi presented Simeon with his first grandchild, a boy who became his namesake. Logan cried watching his father cradle the child in his arms for the first time. Eighteen months later, Naomi delivered a second male child, whom they named Caleb.

During these years, and under his father's tutelage, Logan continued to grow in a knowledge of the Scriptures, until he felt confident enough to instruct his own sons. He remained troubled, however, about the things he'd learned as a child from the New Testament, things that were about to take place in *his* future. Nevertheless, he felt led by the Holy Spirit to keep what he knew locked in his heart.

Eventually, the passage of time took a toll on the relationships Logan had established during his first trip back in time. Three years before Logan's wedding,

Perez married a girl from Bethany and took an aging Eliab to live with them in their house there. A few years later, Jachin contracted leprosy, and despite ardent protests from Ephraim, moved to a remote area in the mountainous regions near Hebron. Zephon remained a bachelor for the remainder of his lifetime, having never married, and passed away eleven years ago. His death was followed by Logan's father four years later. And so, the boy who once complained about missing a meal, wept and fasted for seven days.

Now, Logan returned a wave from Caleb and young Simeon, who'd just appeared over the rise of a smaller hill leading some stray sheep. At the same time, his attention was drawn to the sound of someone calling his name behind him. He turned to see his neighbor, Beriah, ascending the hill using long strides and a quickened pace. "Beriah, my friend," Logan said. "What brings you here in such a hurry?"

Beriah reached the top of the hill and paused to catch his breath. "I just heard. Do you remember the young Rabbi who performed miracles and healed the sick over the past couple of years?"

"Yeshua? Sure. I took the boys to see Him once when he came to Jericho."

"He was just arrested in Jerusalem."

NOTE FROM THE AUTHOR

Dear Reader,

I suspect most writers of inspirational fiction have at least one Christmas story inside them. As proof, I offer the number of holiday-themed titles published each year by my fellow Christian authors. Never one to buck my own theory, *The Boy Who Cried Christmas* is my answer to that calling.

Some of you may have noticed similarities between the part of Logan and the title character from *A Charlie Brown Christmas*. Both are the same age and suffer from the same disillusionment about the true meaning of Christmas. But where Charlie's revelation comes from his hearing of the Christmas story—Linus's memorable recitation from the Gospel of Luke—I wanted Logan to have a more personal experience with the Messiah. Enter the character of Robert, and a journey back to Bethlehem. In using the vehicle of time travel, I not only wanted Logan to *hear* the message of Christmas, but to bring back a firsthand account to share with the world.

My hope is that in reading this book you will be able to experience a small taste of the wonder and excitement, the childlike faith that brought the Christmas story to life for Logan. It's a story that hasn't changed in over two thousand years, despite the best efforts of scoffers to ridicule it.

May the joy of the birth of Christ fill your hearts and homes this holiday season, and for all the years to come.

Merry Christmas,
Dennis

ABOUT THE AUTHOR

Dennis Bailey is a retired police detective who turned in his gun and badge for a monitor and keyboard. He is an ardent student of the Bible who felt the calling of God on his heart to take that learning and use it to further His glory.

He writes suspense-filled, action-packed adventures that feature a touch of the divine. His debut novel, *Army of God*, a story of how the animals of Noah's Ark rose up to defend it against an invading army, was a 2018 finalist for the Blue Ridge Mountains Christian Writers Conference Director's Choice Award, and a Readers' Favorite Gold Medal Award Winner in 2020.

He and his wife, Lee, live in Virginia, where they have a great view of the Blue Ridge Mountains near historic Charlottesville.

If you enjoyed *The Boy Who Cried Christmas*, try my first novel, a Readers' Favorite 2020 Gold Medal Award Winner.

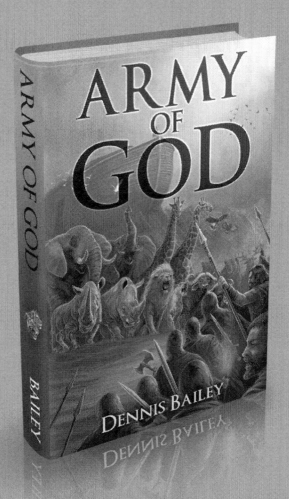

**AVAILABLE NOW IN
BOOKSTORES AND ONLINE**

Made in the USA
Middletown, DE
25 October 2020